## *The Shadow Was Swift and Silent. . . .*

It flowed out from the wall so smoothly that at first all Hannah felt was the crush of fingers against her throat and the merciless strength of a body pressed warm and hard against her back.

"Don't move."

The voice was deep . . . dangerous . . . and as it whispered against her ear, shivers raced wildly down Hannah's spine. She gasped and tried to scream, but the arm around her neck only squeezed tighter, and she could smell mud and wet hair and damp skin.

"One sound," the voice mumbled. "And you won't even know you're dead."

**Books by Richie Tankersley Cusick**

BUFFY, THE VAMPIRE SLAYER
(a novelization based on a screenplay by Joss Whedon)
THE DRIFTER
FATAL SECRETS
HELP WANTED
THE LOCKER
THE MALL
SILENT STALKER
SOMEONE AT THE DOOR
VAMPIRE

Available from ARCHWAY Paperbacks

# RICHIE TANKERSLEY
# CUSICK

Someone at the Door

**AN ARCHWAY PAPERBACK**
Published by POCKET BOOKS
New York  London  Toronto  Sydney  Tokyo  Singapore

This book is a work of fiction. Names, characters, places and incidents are products of the author's imagination or are used fictitiously. Any resemblance to actual events or locales or persons, living or dead, is entirely coincidental.

AN ARCHWAY PAPERBACK *Original*

An Archway Paperback published by
POCKET BOOKS, a division of Simon & Schuster Inc.
1230 Avenue of the Americas, New York, NY 10020

ISBN: 0-671-88742-4

First Archway Paperback printing October 1994

10  9  8  7  6  5  4

AN ARCHWAY PAPERBACK and colophon are
registered trademarks of Simon & Schuster Inc.

Cover art by Lee MacLeod

Printed in the U.S.A.

IL 6+

For Deb,
With love.

*I think that says it all.*

*Someone at the Door*

"This has got to be the coldest January we've ever had," Hannah grumbled, jumping down from the school bus and pulling her jacket tighter. She stomped her feet impatiently and waited for her younger sister to get off behind her. "Hurry up, Meg—I'm half-frozen!"

"Don't get mad at me," Meg replied in an injured tone. "Just 'cause you decided to break up with Kurt today, don't act like it's my—whoops!"

From his seat behind the steering wheel, Ernie Metzer flung out an arm to keep Meg from falling. "Watch out for those steps—they're slippery!" He leaned out toward the open door and squinted off across the snowy landscape, his broad face creased in a frown. "Sure glad this is my last stop. You two think you can make it home okay?"

"No problem." Hannah nodded distractedly. "We're used to wading through snow."

"Been here eight whole months, and talking like natives," Ernie teased. "And I thought you city girls would hate this country life!"

"It's boring," Hannah admitted, but Meg smiled.

"I love it! Especially our house! Did you know it's a hundred years old?"

"What?" Ernie faked surprise. "Almost as old as me!" He chuckled, then added, "There's a good chance you might not have school tomorrow. Just heard the weather report on the radio—predicting a snowstorm to beat all get-out!"

"Great!" Meg clapped her hands. "Maybe we'll get snowed in till Christmas!"

Meg was four years younger than Hannah—a freshman to Hannah's senior status—and no two sisters could have looked less alike. Hannah was tall and athletic; Meg was short and petite. Where Hannah's hair was thick, wavy, and coal-black, offsetting intense brown eyes, Meg's look was more waifish, with a tiny face and limp hair the color of chocolate, and green eyes so big and round that she always looked startled.

*"More* snow?" Hannah grumbled again. "If we get *too* much more, Mom and Dad won't be able to get home."

Ernie cocked his head and wrapped his fingers around the door handle.

"Your folks gone, are they?" he asked, and Meg nodded.

"Our sister-in-law just had a baby, so they went to Colorado to visit everyone. But their plane's due back tonight."

"Better pray the storm holds off, then." Ernie looked genuinely concerned. "Don't like the idea of you girls being way out here by yourselves with more

2

bad weather coming." He frowned again, his eyes sweeping the wooded hillsides and pewter-gray sky. "Heck, *I* don't even like to drive out here in weather like this. All these hills and bad roads—can't think of a worse place to get stuck. Well, you two be careful, now!"

He pulled back into his seat and pulled the door shut after him. The girls saw him raise one hand in a wave, and they stood waving back at him until the bus rumbled out of sight.

"The storm won't be that bad, will it?" Meg asked, lagging behind. "Mom and Dad'll still be able to come home, won't they?"

"Don't ask me. How should I know?" Hannah said irritably. "Anyway, you worry too much."

She moved ahead, but her eyes were busy scanning the soft white shapes around them. Rock piles? Fence posts? Bushes and tree stumps and the old creek bed? Landmarks that had always been so familiar seemed strangely ominous today, camouflaged in their deceptive coatings of snow. Even the road to the house was buried a foot deep, and as the girls trudged toward home, it was hard to tell where the surrounding fields ended and their own yard began.

"So you finally did it," Meg sighed. "Good for you, Hannah. Even though you should have done it a long time ago."

The sound of her sister's voice brought Hannah up sharply. She stopped and turned with a questioning look.

"What are you talking about?" she demanded.

"You know. Kurt."

"Will you drop that, please? I really don't think it's any of your business."

3

Hannah started off again, but Meg fell into step beside her.

"Mom never liked him, you know. Dad either."

"So tell someone who cares," Hannah tossed back, but something caught inside her heart, and she quickly blinked back tears.

"I'm sorry, I didn't mean to hurt your feelings—" Meg began, but Hannah's frown silenced her.

"I don't care what Mom and Dad think," Hannah said angrily. "Breaking up with Kurt didn't have anything to do with Mom and Dad."

"He wasn't ever very nice to you," Meg offered meekly. "He got mad about everything. He didn't like you going places without him, or talking to other guys, or even being with Gilly—"

"Meg, will you just shut up?"

"But Gilly's your best friend! If I had a boyfriend who was jealous of my best friend, I'd tell him to get lost and then I'd—"

"Meg," Hannah said coldly, "you will *never* have a boyfriend. Guys will never like you because you talk way too much, and nothing you say is anything that *anyone* would ever want to hear."

Hannah saw the quick look of hurt on Meg's face, but she moved on before her sister could say anything else. As they reached the top of the hill, there was a loud bark, and a second later a huge black dog lumbered toward them in a flurry of snow.

"Hey, Bruce!" Meg squealed in delight and immediately dropped to her knees, arms spread wide. "Come here, baby!"

Hardly a baby, the Newfoundland galloped awkwardly across the front yard, landing on Meg and rolling with her in the snow. Hannah jumped back with a yell and glared at them.

"You shouldn't do that, Meg—you know it's not good for his arthritis! He's too old to be running around."

"He's not old!" Meg said almost angrily. "And he likes to run! He's glad to see me!" She buried her face in the dog's thick neck and hugged him tightly. "What is it, boy? Did you think we weren't coming home? See, Hannah, he really missed us today."

"It doesn't have anything to do with missing us," Hannah said, brushing herself off. "He's just hungry."

As if to convince her how wrong she was, Bruce stumbled to his feet and butted Hannah's thighs, nearly knocking her down. Then he gazed soulfully up into her face until she finally sighed and gave him a rough scratch behind his ears.

"Okay, okay, I'm sorry," she relented. "But don't start working on me to let you in the house—you know the rules."

She turned and plodded the rest of the way to the front porch, trying to ignore Meg and Bruce as they chased past her. She'd never been that crazy about dogs herself, so when Santa Claus had left the huge black puppy beneath their Christmas tree twelve years ago, she'd been only too happy to let Dad name it and Mom take care of it. But it had been Meg who'd instantly become its best friend, and the two of them had been inseparable ever since. Now, even though Bruce was practically deaf and blind and preferred napping almost more than eating, Meg was the only one in the family who could still coax him to play.

"He's so pathetic," Hannah sighed, as Bruce belly

flopped into a snowdrift and whined for Meg to help him out.

"No, he's not." Meg shoved at his backside, then laughed as Bruce clambered up again onto level ground. "He's still a great watchdog."

"Watchdog, right. He'd stand there and watch while someone robbed our house."

"Well . . ." Meg eyed the big dog lovingly. "He might be old, but he still *looks* ferocious."

"If you can get past all the gray hairs," Hannah mumbled, then on an impulse, reached over to give Bruce a pat on the head. She wouldn't have admitted it for anything, but she was actually kind of glad to see him today. Ever since she'd gotten off the bus, she'd had this strange, uneasy feeling at the back of her mind . . . something she couldn't quite put her finger on. *It's the weather,* she told herself firmly—*just the weather and the storm coming and Mom and Dad being gone, that's all it is. . . .*

"It's so quiet out here today," Meg spoke up behind her, and Hannah jumped.

"What?"

Meg shrugged and looked back at their trail of footprints straggling up the hill through the snow.

"I said it's so quiet out here today. I don't like it."

"Don't start scaring yourself," Hannah said curtly, shoving her key into the front door, turning the knob. "You and that wild imagination of yours."

"Mom says I'm just creative," Meg protested as Hannah pushed her into the hall and closed the door behind them. They could hear Bruce whining and scratching to be let in, and Hannah shrugged out of her coat and headed for the kitchen.

"Can't we just—" Meg began, but Hannah shook her head adamantly.

"No, his doghouse is plenty warm. Besides, Mom would have a fit if she knew Bruce was in here. He'll tear everything up."

"No, he won't. I'll make sure he stays in the kitchen."

Even as Meg was talking, Hannah did a quick survey of the room, mentally calculating all the things Bruce could destroy—the wooden countertops and cupboards (he'd already managed to scratch those up just by standing on his hind legs), the towel rack (he'd shredded two dish towels and Mom's favorite apron one morning when Mom's back was turned), the door to the back porch (he'd gnawed the doorframe away twice), the kitchen table (he'd broken a platter and made off with a whole lemon chiffon cake on Dad's birthday), and the door to the storeroom (which, even though it was shut off and never used, was an intriguing source of mouse noises, which made Bruce bark and howl at the top of his lungs and butt the door till he was addle-headed).

"I promise," Meg tried again. "I really will—"

"You will not. You'll sneak him upstairs, and I'll get in trouble because I'm supposed to be in charge."

"If he does anything bad, I'll tell Mom it was my idea and you didn't know."

"How could I not know? He's as big as an elephant."

The phone rang, interrupting their argument, and Hannah answered with an angry "What?" Meg went to the living room and switched on the TV, deliberately turning it louder as Hannah tried to talk.

"What?" Hannah said again, pressing her palm to her other ear, yelling at Meg to turn down the volume. "What? Hello?"

"It's me," said a familiar voice. "You guys still alone over there?"

"Oh, hi, Gilly." As Meg wandered back in, Hannah made a grab for her, but Meg expertly ducked out of reach. "Just a minute, okay?"

"Sure, just put me on hold," Gilly teased. "I'm just your best friend, *I* certainly don't matter."

"Meg," Hannah gritted her teeth, "if you don't—"

Meg turned her back and started rummaging in the refrigerator. Hannah heard Gilly talking again, and squeezed the receiver against her ear.

"What? What did you say?"

"I said, are you surviving the big breakup?" Gilly said sympathetically. "The whole school was talking about it today. As if you didn't know."

"It was horrible," Hannah admitted, feeling the heaviness in her heart again. "He didn't take it well at all."

"Surprise, surprise."

"But it had to be done."

"Who are you trying to convince, me or you?"

"Kurt and I've been going together for almost six months—it's not like this was the easiest thing I ever had to do!"

"But you *did* do it. And I know how hard it was."

Hannah nodded, certain that Gilly in her typical best-friend fashion could see her face and feel her pain.

"If I were you, I'd keep my doors locked," Gilly went on, not unkindly. "You know how Kurt is."

"Oh, come on, he wouldn't do anything to me," Hannah said with more confidence than she felt. "And anyway, he's going on that ski trip this weekend. He won't even be around."

"If you're lucky. I mean it, Han, you know that terrible temper of his. Rejection's never been one of his strong points."

Hannah pulled a kitchen chair over and slowly sank down onto it.

"There must be at least fifty girls chomping at the bit for Kurt to ask them out," she said unhappily. "He's not going to waste his time getting even with me when he can have his pick of any girl in the whole school."

"You're rationalizing." There was a brief silence, then Gilly went on carefully. "Look, Han, everyone knows how mean Kurt can be when he's mad. You've humiliated him by breaking it off . . . made him look bad in front of his stupid macho friends. I don't know why you ever got mixed up with him in the first place."

Hannah closed her eyes, her throat aching with tears. *Because he's the cutest guy at school, not to mention the star quarterback—because he chose me out of everyone else, because we were the most popular couple, because being Kurt's girlfriend made me feel pretty and popular and powerful and—*

"Hannah?" Gilly sounded anxious. "Are you all right?"

"Yes," she sighed. "I'm all right. Gilly—"

"Oh, Hannah, I'm sorry, I shouldn't have said what I did. I know you feel terrible. And even though we talked about you doing this a million times, it's still got to hurt like crazy, even though we both know it's absolutely right. You couldn't go on with a crazy person like Kurt—it's just not healthy. Or safe."

"Don't remind me."

"Well, I *am* going to remind you so you'll feel better about yourself," Gilly said sternly. "Just remember how Kurt got arrested for beating David up, just 'cause David asked you to help him study. And how Kurt got hauled in for trying to run Steve off the road just 'cause Steve gave you a ride home a couple weeks ago. And all those other times Kurt got—"

"I said don't remind me."

"The guy's got a mind like a steel trap. He *doesn't* forget. That's what *really* scares me. He remembers every single person and every single thing that ever upset him in his whole life. And then he gets revenge —no matter how long it takes."

"This is supposed to make me feel better?"

"Hannah, please be careful. Are your folks home yet?"

"No, not till tonight."

*"I'll* feel better when they're with you."

"Gilly, there's so much snow out this way, no one in their right mind would try coming out here!"

"And who says Kurt's in his right mind?"

"I've got Meg and Bruce."

"Wow. *That's* a relief."

In spite of herself, Hannah laughed. In the background the TV blared even louder, and she swiveled around in her chair to yell again at Meg.

"Listen!" Meg shouted at her, and as Hannah opened her mouth to shout back, she heard the voice of the TV newsman blaring from the living room.

"—escaped early this afternoon from Fairway Institution. He was last spotted in a heavily wooded area outside Ansonville, and is believed to be heading south."

"Hannah," Meg began, but Hannah shushed her.

"Be quiet, Meg! Listen!"

"—murderer was sentenced twenty years ago to the state hospital for the criminally insane. He is considered armed and extremely dangerous. If you have any information about this man, notify the authorities immediately. Do not—repeat, *do not*—attempt to apprehend him—"

"Hannah?" Gilly's voice came insistently over the phone. "Hannah, are you there? What's going on?"

"He killed four guards and got away." Meg's eyes were as big as saucers, and she could barely choke out the words. "They think he got hurt trying to escape, but they don't know how bad. And then he forced his way into a woman's car—and they found the woman dead—"

"Hannah?" Gilly yelled. "Hey, Hannah!"

"They think he might be on foot now, hiding out in the woods." Meg took a step toward her sister, oblivious to the game show blaring now from the TV. "Oh, Hannah—if they're right, that means he's heading this way!"

**2**

"Hannah!" Gilly shouted. "Hello?"

Hannah fumbled the receiver back to her ear. This time when she motioned Meg to turn down the television, her sister nodded and left the room.

"Gilly, have you heard anything about an escaped mental patient?" Hannah asked anxiously.

"No, why?"

"There was just something about it on TV."

"From Fairway? That's miles from here. So what?"

"So I'm going to see if there's anything else on about it—call you later."

Hannah hung up the phone. She heard Meg turn the TV off, and as her younger sister stared at her from the hallway, silence surged through the kitchen like a giant wave.

"Oh, for heaven's sake," Hannah said irritably. "One stupid news report and you get all hysterical. That's so like you, Meg."

12

"I'm not hysterical." Meg's voice sounded very small. "I was just listening, that's all."

"I don't know why you even turn on the news anyway," Hannah grumbled. "You always get upset over everything bad that happens."

"I do not."

"Yes, you do. You start imagining all the worst possible things."

"I do *not!* I turned the TV off, didn't I? You're the one who said you were going to find out more about that report."

"Just so you won't drive me crazy all night being scared."

"You're the one who's driving people crazy. Just 'cause you broke up with your stupid boyfriend doesn't mean the rest of the world has to suffer along with you."

Before Hannah could reply, Meg gathered up her books and flounced out of the room. A moment later Hannah heard her go upstairs and slam her bedroom door.

For a long time Hannah just sat there.

She thought about the look on Meg's face when the news report had been on, and she thought about the urgency in the announcer's voice. She put her hands over her face and shook her head.

"I don't need this," she groaned.

She got up and went into the living room and turned on the TV again. The game show was getting wilder, and she quickly switched channels. A talk show. A commercial for cat food. A science fiction movie. A soap opera. A group of people shouting at each other about politics. Hannah clicked through the whole remote and finally ended up with cartoons.

The phone rang again, and Hannah automatically reached for the extension on the end table, laughing as she answered.

"Okay, Gilly, what did you forget to tell me?"

"I'm going to kill you," the voice hissed.

Ice shot through Hannah's veins. She pressed the receiver to her ear and fought to keep her voice steady.

"Kurt?" she demanded. "Kurt—is that you?"

"You're seeing someone else, aren't you?" the voice said venomously. "Going out on me, aren't you, you—"

"Stop it! Don't you dare talk to me that way!" Hannah bolted upright, her voice trembling with rage and panic. "You've been drinking, haven't you? And if you're trying to scare me, you can just forget it—I'm *not scared* of you!"

"I know you and Meg are alone. I know your parents are gone, and I know how long and dark that drive is to the airport when you go to pick them up tonight—"

"You don't know anything, Kurt! Don't you ever call me again!"

"You're not going to get away with it," the voice went on, and this time it laughed, a laugh that sent chills up Hannah's spine. "You hear me, Hannah? I'll kill you before I'll let anyone else have you."

Kurt hung up.

Thoroughly shaken, Hannah clutched the phone tightly in her fist and stared unseeingly at the television. *My God, he really is crazy. . . . Why did I ever wait so long to end this mess?*

Slowly she put the receiver down. She wrapped her arms around herself and cried softly. But of course, he wouldn't really try anything, she argued to herself. He was just upset, that's all, and he always got belligerent when he was mad. Besides, no one would be stupid enough to go out in weather like this. . . .

Wiping her tears, Hannah stretched out on the couch and stared across the room to the large front window. She could see the ice-coated branches of the old oak tree that towered beside the porch, and she could see the ponderous gray sky that showed in between, quilted with ominous snow clouds. Her eyes roamed around the cozy room, from overstuffed chairs to cluttered bookshelves to the brick fireplace. Suddenly it didn't seem quite so cozy, quite so safe as it always had before. . . .

She made a mental note to bring in more firewood before it started snowing again. She fastened her eyes on the television screen, but it was all a blur, and the drone of the TV was hypnotic. Hannah could feel her eyelids getting heavy. She shifted into a more comfortable position on the deep, soft cushions, and tried to distract her mind. *Don't think about what just happened. . . . It's only Kurt having one of his tantrums. Dinner . . . yes, dinner. Whose turn is it tonight, Meg's or mine?* Hannah knew it didn't really matter—she could always bully Meg into doing anything she wanted her to do. *Well, it's her own fault,* Hannah reminded herself, willing away a tiny twinge of guilt. *If Meg weren't so wishy-washy, then she wouldn't get stuck with everything.*

It started to snow. Lying there, Hannah saw them floating past the windowpane—big, wet flakes—but like the background noise of the TV, they were strangely soothing, lulling her into a doze. *I can't tell Meg about that phone call. . . . I can't waste time worrying about such a stupid, idiotic threat.* She stared at the snowflakes from some restful twilight state, feeling herself drift off, and the flakes grew bigger and bigger, and then thicker, until the whole window was one solid blur of swirling whiteness. . . .

Hannah woke with a start.

Had the telephone rung? Nothing was ringing now, but from some remote corner of her mind she thought she heard a voice, loud and insistent, and some instinct told her she should be paying attention. She struggled into a sitting position just in time to see an image flash off the TV screen, just in time to hear the reporter say, "And if you see this man, do not attempt to apprehend him. Notify your local police immediately."

"Damn!" Hannah grabbed the remote and clicked hurriedly through the other networks, but all she got was commercials. Angrily she realized that the disappearing image must have been a picture of that escaped killer, and she'd missed the whole thing, update and all. She started through the whole series of channels once more, when suddenly the TV burst into loud static, and the screen went white.

"Meg!" she shouted. "Is the TV working in Mom and Dad's room?"

Tossing the remote on the table, Hannah got up, then froze as her eyes fell on the front window. To her surprise, it looked almost identical to the TV screen—a cloudy square of pale fuzziness—as though the whole world beyond had turned to static. Uneasily she hurried up the stairs and opened the door to Meg's room.

"Meg, did you hear me? I—"

She broke off when she saw Meg with the telephone. Her younger sister was perched on the side of the bed, and Hannah could tell she was upset. Hannah walked over to stand beside her, and Meg immediately handed over the receiver.

"It's Mom," Meg said. "They're not coming home."

"What?" Hannah cringed as crackling burst over the line. "Hello? Mom? Can you hear me?"

"Hannah, is that you?" Mrs. Stuart's voice was faint, and Hannah had to strain to hear. "We're— airport—snowed in—"

"What?" Hannah talked louder, forcing calm into her voice. "Mom? I can hardly hear you—"

"Don't know—when—home—"

"What?"

"Snow—terrible—sorry—"

"Mom, I can't hear you—"

"Take care—let you know—"

"But when—"

"—love you—"

"Mom?"

Hannah held the phone away as the line popped like miniature fireworks. She listened a few minutes more, but there was nothing at all.

"It's dead," she sighed, handing it back to Meg. "The lines must be down."

"Was that Mom who called earlier?" Meg fretted.

Hannah avoided her sister's eyes. "When?"

"I don't know. A while ago. Didn't you answer it?"

"Oh. That. Wrong number."

Meg walked slowly over to the window and peered out into the swirling darkness. "It's not just snowing out there. There's ice coming down, too."

And Hannah could hear it now—tiny pellets against the windowpane. She stared down at Meg's history book open on the bedspread, and then she gathered herself together with an effort.

"How come you didn't wake me?"

"I thought you needed to sleep," Meg said quietly. "I know you had a terrible day."

Hannah felt a lump rise in her throat. She swallowed hard and forced it back down.

"Maybe we should let Bruce in," she said at last.

Meg turned and faced her. Sheepishly she pointed to her closet where a huge pile of dirty clothes lay just inside the half-open door.

"I already did," she sighed.

As Hannah watched, the pile of dirty clothes rose up from the floor and shook itself—socks, sweatshirts, and underwear spraying out in all directions. Bruce cocked his head and looked beseechingly at Hannah, one white sock draped over his ear and across his face like a pirate with an eye patch.

Hannah burst out laughing. Meg joined in, and Bruce clambered up onto the bed, tail wagging ecstatically.

"Just for that, *you* can fix dinner," Hannah ordered, heading downstairs with Meg and Bruce close behind.

"I thought you'd say that." Meg sounded almost smug. "So I already did that, too."

Even Hannah had to admit it was good. As she sat at the table eating her second bowl of chili and trying to ignore Bruce's head on her lap, the lights suddenly flickered overhead, plunging the kitchen in and out of shadow.

"Is the electricity going out?" Meg spun around from the sink, her big eyes widening. "Oh, Hannah, we'll freeze to death!"

"We won't freeze, dummy, we have a gas heater," Hannah said, with more confidence than she felt. Had it just been a week ago she'd heard her parents talking about that ancient furnace and how it needed to be replaced before it breathed its last breath? She got up and rummaged in a lower cabinet, pulling out two flashlights. "Let's keep these handy, just in case. And I'll get some lanterns from the garage."

Meg nodded. "I saw Dad fill them before he left."

"And let's build a fire. We can always sleep down here if we have to. We have plenty of wood."

"And blankets," Meg reminded her. "And Bruce. Between the three of us, we should stay nice and warm."

The girls pulled on their coats and opened the back door, bracing themselves as an icy blast roared through the kitchen. Bruce bolted out, disappearing at once into the storm, and after propping the door open so Meg could lug in firewood from the porch, Hannah ran for the garage. The small building stood apart from the house—behind and a little to one side—and it took a while to plow her way over. The backyard was a solid sheet of white, bordered at the rear by a heavy tree line and densely wooded hills beyond. Already the tree limbs were thickening, matting together with ice. Hannah burrowed deeper into her coat and glanced at the woodpile as she passed. She could still see the huge mound of logs, ready to be brought in, and the broad tree stump alongside with the axe embedded in its surface. But even these were fast disappearing in the steady fall of snow.

Drifts had piled up against the front of the garage, so Hannah tried the normal door at the back. When it wouldn't open at first, she leaned her whole weight against it, then cried out in surprise as it gave way and spilled her in on the concrete floor.

The garage was like an icebox. The one high window in here was too tiny and dirty to ever let in light, and was a year-round source of drafts. As Hannah stumbled to her feet, she shone her flashlight around the murky interior and saw her breath crystallizing in front of her face. Shivering, she made her way toward the back to her dad's workbench. There were shelves hanging above, and after several sweeps of her light, she found the lanterns and pulled them down.

Something moved in the darkness behind her.

Gasping, Hannah spun around, her flashlight making a crazy arc across the ceiling and floor. Her parents' station wagon took up most of the space, and as she played the thin beam of light over it, it looked like some predatory beast crouching there, glass eyes bugged out, fender lips spread wide in a fiendish grin.

In slow awareness, Hannah realized she was pressed back against the workbench, the edge of the table digging hard into her spine. Wincing, she pulled away and aimed her flashlight into the shadows that crept along the walls. Mom had been after them forever to clean their junk out of here—so why hadn't they done it? Hannah wondered now. There was so much clutter, it would be easy for someone to hide . . . to blend in with the rest of the shadows. . . .

As the wind lifted in a mournful wail, Hannah felt the hair rise along the back of her neck.

Before her very eyes one of the shadows started to grow . . . to spread itself out into a human shape . . . to sink down again into nothingness. . . .

"Oh, God," Hannah whispered.

She couldn't move. Every single nerve was paralyzed. As she stood there helplessly frozen, the shadow moved again, rising slowly into the air. Hannah couldn't take her eyes off it. Without warning the horrible thing burst from the darkness and flapped toward her like a giant bat.

Hannah shrieked and thrust her light forward. The thing fluttered onto the hood of the car, and Hannah stared at it in dismay.

*A shirt . . . It's just an old shirt. . . .*

Swallowing a sob, Hannah let herself slide down the garage wall into a sitting position. Her body felt weak and sick, and she buried her face in her hands.

*A shirt. I nearly had a heart attack over a stupid shirt. . . .*

Of course, she should have remembered. Mom was always sticking things out here for that garage sale she was always going to have someday. *She must have put some bags of clothes out here, and some of them spilled out, and when the wind gusted in through the cracks, it caught one of the shirts and swooped it straight up in the air.*

*I'm glad Meg didn't see this—I'd never live it down.*

Determinedly Hannah got to her feet, took the lanterns, and went back to the house. Bruce was digging in the driveway, and she just managed to keep from falling over him as he spun around to greet her. For the next twenty minutes the girls carried firewood from the backyard to the porch, then gathered up a stash of candles, flashlights, and lamps. By the time they finished, both of them were exhausted, and after checking all the doors and windows, they went up to bed.

"Guess I don't have to worry about setting the

alarm clock," Hannah sighed, as Meg paused in her own doorway. "I don't imagine anyone'll be going to school."

"I wish the TV would come back on," Meg said wistfully. "It's a perfect night to watch old movies."

"You'd just cry," Hannah reminded her.

Meg nodded distractedly, started into her room, then turned back to her sister.

"Hannah?"

"What?"

"Don't you think it's kind of strange that Kurt hasn't tried to get ahold of you?"

A stab went through Hannah's heart. She hoped her voice sounded normal.

"The phones are out, Meg."

"That's not exactly what I meant."

In spite of the warm, safe house, Hannah felt a shiver ripple through to her bones.

"I broke up with him, remember? There's no *reason* for him to get ahold of me."

"But that's just it. Whenever you've tried to stand up to him before, he never takes no for an answer. He always bothers you till you give in."

"Harasses me, you mean," Hannah said shortly. "Well, maybe this time he's not going to bother, because he knows I *won't* give in. I think I made it pretty clear today how I feel."

Meg nodded, but her face still looked troubled. "Yeah . . . okay . . . I guess so." She lifted her eyes to Hannah's face and forced a smile. "I *hope* so."

"See you in the morning," Hannah told her, and stood there till Meg's door closed. Then she stared down both ends of the hallway and down the shadowy staircase, and then she shivered again and shut herself in her room.

*Oh, Meg, if you only knew . . .*

Hannah leaned against her door and closed her eyes, biting her lip in frustration. No, it wasn't like Kurt to give up his possessions without a fight—and Hannah had always been one of his most prized possessions. It had taken her a long time to realize exactly what she was worth in Kurt's eyes— something to own, to boss around and brag about, and not much more—but the privilege of being Kurt's girl had been more important than anything else in the beginning.

*Why did it take me this long to break it off—I'm such an idiot. . . .*

She could still see his face—how he'd looked today when she'd told him. The anger and arrogance and— yes—the absolute hatred in his eyes. If it hadn't been broad daylight and if the school hadn't been full of kids and teachers, she would have panicked and run for her life.

Yes, she thought miserably, Meg was certainly right about Kurt. It wasn't like him to give up without a fight—and he could be a nasty fighter.

*He just wanted to scare me, that's all. He just wanted to bully me one last time. . . .*

Forcing the thoughts from her mind, Hannah showered, put on her flannel nightgown, and climbed into bed. She lay awake in the dark a long time. Around her the house creaked and trembled in the thrashing wind, and snow beat mercilessly at the windowpanes. She huddled down beneath piles of blankets and tried to concentrate on happy things . . . silly things . . . but the images wouldn't come. She even thought about going to Meg's room, but knew her sister would be fast asleep by now, buried beneath the warm furry layers of Bruce.

So it surprised her when she suddenly heard Meg's voice calling her name—surprised her and made her think she must have dozed off after all, must have been dreaming, because Meg looked so real standing there in her bedroom doorway, silhouetted against the pale light of the hall. . . .

"Hannah?" Meg's voice was shaking, and she sounded like she might cry. "Hannah—wake up!"

And as Hannah pushed back the covers and swung her feet to the floor, she heard something else— something faint but unmistakable—a pounding that echoed up from the downstairs hall—

"Hannah," Meg said again, and her face was as white as a ghost. "Do you hear it? Someone's at the door!"

# 3

For a second it seemed to Hannah that everything froze.

She could see the terrified mask of Meg's face. She could see Bruce stiffening at Meg's side . . . could hear the low growl building in his throat as he sensed their fear, even though Hannah knew he couldn't possibly hear a thing.

"Who do you think it is?" Meg whispered, and Hannah glanced at the clock on her nightstand.

Two A.M.

*Two in the morning in a totally isolated place miles away from everything—just Meg and me and this stupid dog all alone in the house in the middle of a snowstorm—*

"Hannah," Meg whispered again. "What are we going to do?"

Downstairs the pounding grew louder. Hannah snatched up the phone by her bed and listened to the

25

empty silence on the line. Meg twined her fists into Bruce's hair, and the dog whined nervously.

"It must be someone we know, right?" Meg went on, her eyes filling the tiny contours of her face. "I mean, no one even knows we live out here except for our friends, right? It must be someone we know—"

"Turn off that light," Hannah said, pushing past Meg out into the hall. "Get Bruce to bark."

"What?"

"You heard me—make him bark!"

Hannah flapped her arms at Bruce, who immediately dropped to the floor and let loose with a booming yelp.

"He thinks you're playing." Meg wrung her hands. "He thinks you're—"

"Get one of his toys!"

Meg dashed back into her bedroom, returning a second later with Bruce's favorite ball. She flung it down the stairs, and as Bruce hurled himself after it, the sisters ran after him into the front hall.

"Maybe they'll think we're not home!" Meg whimpered. "Maybe they'll just go away and leave us—"

"Shh!"

The pounding had stopped, but it was finally beginning to dawn on Bruce that something was wrong. Throwing himself at the front door, he attacked it with a vengeance, trying to get at whatever was on the other side. The girls pressed back against the wall, and as Bruce continued his deafening attack, a voice shouted above the confusion.

"Hello? Is anyone home? We need help!"

The girls froze. Hannah felt Meg's fingers digging

into her arm, and she bit her lip to keep from crying out in pain.

"Can anyone hear me?" the voice yelled again.

Bruce's huge feet raked down the door, shredding wood, and his barks grew angry and wild. Meg clamped her hands over her ears, and Hannah put one arm around her sister's shoulder, hugging her close.

"Please!" the voice begged. "We need help out here!"

"What if something's really wrong?" Meg whispered fearfully. "What if—"

*"Shh!"* Hannah hissed again, holding Meg tighter. Maybe Meg was right—if the two of them just stood here long enough, maybe whoever was out there would think no one was home and go away. She could feel her breath about to explode in her throat. The doorknob rattled violently, and her eyes fastened in on the dead bolt above it.

"Are they coming in?" Meg choked. "Oh, Hannah, I think they're coming—"

Something thudded against the door. Keeping her hand over Meg's mouth, Hannah dragged her sister into the deep shadows of the hallway. *This isn't going to work—they think nobody's home, so they're going to break in—*

"Please help us!" the muffled voice called again, and even to Hannah's ears it was sounding weaker. "Won't anyone help . . . ?"

"I can't stand this, Hannah!" Meg cried. "We can't just leave somebody out there!"

Without warning Meg twisted free and ran for the door. Hannah gave a warning shout, but before she could move, there was an icy blast and the hall was filled with stinging, swirling snow.

"Meg!" Hannah yelled.

But it was too late.

Even as she started forward, she could see the two figures silhouetted there in the front doorway . moving across the threshold into the house.

28

# 4

For a split second Hannah felt only disbelief.

From some faraway place she could hear Bruce barking and Meg's terrified screams, and then, to her horror, one of the shadowy figures stumbled forward and fell to the floor.

"Close the door!" Hannah ordered. "Turn on the lights!"

The wind shut off with a whoosh. A second later the overhead fixture burst on, and as Hannah blinked against the sudden brightness, the hallway came into focus at last.

A young man was lying at her feet.

He was so pale, so still, that all Hannah could do was stare.

"Is he . . . is he dead?" Meg whispered.

Hannah shook her head and knelt beside him. He was lying on his back, arms flung out to either side, jeans and sweater and coat soaking wet. Snow crusted the long black hair that flowed around his head and shoulders, and in the glaring light, tiny crystals of ice glistened in his dark lashes against the bluish pallor of his skin. There was a jagged slash across his forehead, stiff with dried blood. He couldn't have been much over eighteen, Hannah decided—twenty at the most —and as she felt him stir slightly beneath her touch, she jerked her hand back again.

"Hannah," Meg whispered, "look . . ."

As Hannah glanced up, she suddenly remembered the second figure that had come into the house—the second someone who was even now trapped in the corner beside the front door while Bruce stood guard, growling deep in his throat.

"Who are you!" Hannah jumped to her feet, wedging herself between Meg and the stranger. "What are you doing here?"

Bruce, feeling Hannah's touch on his neck, struck out for the corner with a vicious, well-aimed snap. To Hannah's amazement, there was a ripping sound, followed by an exclamation of pain, and the stranger held up both hands in surrender.

"Come on, call him off! I'm not going to hurt you—"

"Who *are* you!" Hannah demanded again. She looked down at his thigh and the shreds of wet fabric hanging from his jeans. Bruce quivered and poised for another attack.

"Jonathon," the stranger said hoarsely. "My name is . . . Jonathon. Please . . ." He nodded at the figure on the floor. "Just help him, okay?"

Hannah slid her fingers inside Bruce's collar and slowly tightened her grip. The dog glanced at her for some sign of encouragement, but after a long hesitation, she finally shook her head.

"Sit, Bruce," she mumbled, tugging on him. "Good dog."

Unwillingly Bruce sat. Hannah narrowed her eyes and studied the second young man as he slid down and squatted on the floor.

He looked to be about the same age as his companion, the same tall height and slenderness, but with slightly narrower shoulders, and more fair than dark. A shock of pale hair fell over his forehead, and as he brushed it back, Hannah could see the startling blue of his eyes.

"He hit his head," Jonathon murmured, his own eyes drooping shut. "He's half-frozen. . . ."

Hannah continued to stare. Behind her she heard Meg speak up shakily.

"We can't call a doctor. The phones are out."

Jonathon's eyes opened again. They settled on Hannah.

"If we could stay here," he said softly. "Just till the storm lets up . . ."

Hannah's mind raced. Her eyes flicked from Meg to the floor, then back again to the boy in the corner.

"What happened to you?" she asked.

Jonathon's shoulders moved slightly beneath the soggy weight of his denim jacket. Hannah gazed down at his torn, wet jeans and realized for the first time that the dark stains were blood, and that drops of it were spattering the floor around his boot.

"You're bleeding!" she said, and fear made her tone more angry than sympathetic. She glanced at Bruce, but Jonathon shook his head.

"No . . . no . . . the dog didn't do it—"

"What *happened* to you? What are you doing out here in the middle of—"

"Car . . ." For the first time a faint whisper came from the floor. As Hannah knelt beside the dark-haired boy, she could barely see his lips move. "Get out of . . . road . . . brid . . ."

His voice trailed away. Hannah felt for his pulse, relieved when it stirred weakly beneath her fingertips.

"What did he say?" Hannah looked back at the boy in the corner, who was staring wearily at his companion.

"He said bridge. My car skidded off a bridge into the water. We've been walking. . . ."

"Bridge?" Meg echoed in alarm. "There's only one bridge around here—over on County Line Road. That's two miles away!"

"We've been walking," Jonathon went on. "Looking for help . . . a house . . . but there's nothing. Nothing for miles and miles and . . ."

His voice trailed off. His eyes shifted from Hannah to Meg to the motionless body of his friend, and then he heaved himself wearily to his feet.

"Look . . . I know you two are scared—strangers showing up like this in the middle of the night. There's absolutely no reason you should trust us or believe us or even take us in. But if you *won't* help, I'll have to find someone who can. We'll have to go somewhere else."

Hannah watched as Jonathon's hand went slowly to his leg. His cheeks tightened in pain, and his fingertips turned wet with blood. She saw the frantic look on Meg's face. She heard the shriek of the wind as it pelted the house with snow.

"Hannah," Meg whispered, and Hannah put her hands to her ears, trying to shut out her sister's voice. *Oh, Meg, I know you're scared—I am, too, that's why we have to let them go—we have to let them go right now while we're still safe—*

She could see the confusion in Meg's eyes, could see Meg's mouth silently forming the words *What are we going to do?* and Hannah stared back at her, trying to direct her own thoughts straight into Meg's brain—

*We're going to let them go, do you understand—we don't know who they are—we don't know what they're doing out here at this hour in this weather—don't you realize the danger—they have to go right now, even if they're hurt—they have to go somewhere else—*

"There isn't anywhere else," Hannah heard Meg say.

For a long moment there was silence. Hannah gazed down at the boy on the floor, at the white snow melting and pooling around his dark, dark hair.

"Hannah," Meg whispered again, "there *isn't* anywhere else. They'll die—"

"Get the beds ready," Hannah said abruptly, and she sounded like a stranger to herself, some unfamiliar girl speaking from a long way off. "And find as many blankets as you can."

"Beds?" Meg squeaked. "Whose beds?"

Hannah pointed to the motionless figure beside her. "We'll put him in the king-size. Jonathon can have yours."

"Mine!"

"You heard me!" Hannah stood up and grabbed her sister's arm, pressing close to Meg's ear. "What do you *expect* me to do with them?" she hissed. "I *can't* turn

33

them out now! It was *your* idea to let them in—I hope you're satisfied!"

Gritting her teeth, Hannah gave Meg a shove, then turned back to the task at hand. Jonathon was watching her, shifting his weight awkwardly from one foot to the other. Once more a muscle flinched in his cheek, but his voice came out steady and calm.

"Really . . . we don't want to cause any trouble—"

"Just help me get him upstairs," Hannah said sharply. "Do you think you can?"

He hesitated . . . nodded. "Show me where."

*This can't be happening—can't be—what am I going to do—what else* can *I do—*

"—your parents." Jonathon's voice sounded softly in her ear, and Hannah whirled with a gasp.

"What did you say?"

She hadn't heard him leave the corner, hadn't even heard him cross the hall. Now his blue eyes gazed into hers, and as he leaned forward, one sleeve lightly touched her arm.

"Your parents," he spoke again. "Don't you think you should wake them up?"

And it came to her then, in a slow, chilling realization, that he *knew* her parents weren't here—that he knew she and Meg were completely alone—that somehow, *somehow* he knew—

"They're . . ."

She couldn't say it. She turned away, her mind racing furiously.

"So when will they be back?" he asked.

This time Hannah met his eyes. She faced him squarely, her chin lifted and jaw set, her voice hard and surprisingly composed.

"I don't know. They're stranded at the airport because of the storm. But until they *do* get back, *I'm* in charge."

Was that the faintest smile at the corners of his mouth—or some other emotion she couldn't quite read? Before Hannah could decide, Jonathon lowered his head.

"Of course you are," he mumbled. "I didn't doubt that for a second."

He looked up again and stared at her—blue, blue eyes so deep and so soft that Hannah had the sudden sensation of being drawn into them against her will. She could feel her heart hammering in her chest, but she forced herself to stare back.

"Follow me," she directed.

She led the way to the second floor. Halfway up the stairs, she paused to look back and saw him struggling to keep up. He was limping badly, trying to support his friend's weight with one shoulder, a smear of blood trailing him down the hall.

Hannah stood and watched for several minutes, then swore under her breath.

"Here," she muttered, going back down, "let me help."

Jonathon seemed surprised by her offer. He managed to steady himself, but then shook his head. "No, it's okay, I can manage."

"Don't be stupid," Hannah told him. "You're bleeding all over the floor."

Before Jonathon could argue any further, she propped herself beneath his companion's other arm, and together they managed to drag him to the bedroom. Meg had already turned on the light and pulled down the covers. As Jonathon lowered his friend onto the bed, Hannah began rummaging in her father's closet.

"If we could just warm him up," Jonathon said worriedly. "That's the most important—"

"You better get his clothes off," Hannah broke in. "He needs to get out of those wet things." Glancing over her shoulder, she briefly met Jonathon's eyes, then looked away. "You, too," she added. "Before you both catch pneumonia."

"I'm okay," Jonathon mumbled.

"You're not okay. And your leg—"

"I said I'm fine," he snapped.

Jonathon straightened, the lines of his face going tight and pale. Hannah looked back at him, then slowly moved toward the hall, where Meg and Bruce stood waiting.

"He needs to get warm," Jonathon mumbled again, stripping off the other boy's coat and sweater. "That's all we can do for him right now . . . just get him warm. . . ."

Hannah stared at the figure sprawled on her parents' bed. She could feel Meg shivering against her back.

"You don't need to stay," Jonathon added, but his tone softened a little. "I'll be with him. You should get some sleep."

"The bathroom's through there." Hannah nodded, indicating the connecting door. "You can sleep in the room across the hall if you want." On impulse she drew herself up stiffly. "But don't go anywhere else in the house. Strangers make Bruce very nervous, and I can't be responsible for what he might do to you."

Jonathon didn't answer. He tossed the wet sweater

into a corner and looked at the clothes Hannah had laid at the foot of the bed.

"And you have to leave in the morning," Hannah said.

Behind her she heard Meg's quick intake of breath. Across the room Jonathon hesitated but didn't look up.

"Both of you." Hannah wrapped her fingers around the doorknob and squeezed hard to keep from shaking. "As soon as the snow lets up. The road crews will be out here early, you know . . . to make sure we're all right."

Jonathon stared down at his companion. He stared for several long seconds, and then at last his eyes climbed slowly to meet Hannah's.

"As isolated as you are?" he murmured. "I don't think so."

# 5

"Are we going to die?" Meg's eyes filled with tears as Hannah shoved her into the bedroom and locked the door behind her.

"Turn on my radio," Hannah ordered. "And keep it down."

"Are we going to—"

"Shut up, Meg—I'm trying to think!"

Hannah pushed past her and began searching through the bookshelves by her desk.

"The radio, Meg—where's my radio!"

She gave Bruce a shove up onto her bed and snatched the phone from her nightstand. After listening a second into the receiver, she slammed it down again, then turned impatiently to see her sister standing wide-eyed by the window.

"It's not here," Meg mumbled. "I . . . kind of borrowed it."

"You know my stuff's off-limits—go get it!"

"Well, what I mean is . . . I sort of took it to school for that speech I had to give. . . .." Meg's voice quivered. "And . . . I guess I forgot it."

Hannah slammed her fist against the wall. A jolt of pain shot through her, and with a gasp, she sat down hard on the edge of the bed and cradled her hand against her chest.

"I'm sorry, Hannah," Meg whispered.

For a long time neither girl spoke. Bruce whined and snuggled into the blankets, eyeing both of them warily.

"Oh, Meg," Hannah sighed, covering her face with her hands. "What are we going to do?"

Again the silence stretched out. Hannah closed her eyes, while hundreds of gory thoughts swirled out of control through her brain.

"We couldn't just let them die," Meg spoke up at last. "Could we?"

Hannah spread her fingers apart, staring out between them at her sister.

"I mean, people *do* get lost." Meg tried to keep her voice reasonable. "People do get stranded and have accidents late at night in bad weather. If Mom and Dad were here, they would have taken them in."

Hannah said nothing. Meg went on.

"If you hadn't heard that report on the radio, you wouldn't even be thinking anything bad or scary. If you hadn't heard about that escaped killer, I bet you wouldn't even be afraid—"

"Of course I'd be afraid—are you crazy?" Hannah took her hands from her face and began counting off on her fingertips. "There are two strange guys in our house, Meg—right across the hall from us with nothing but a locked door to keep them out. We don't know anything about them—who they are, where they're from, or what they're doing here. One of them just admitted he *knows* how alone we are. And the other one just happens to be unconscious and could end up dying in Mom and Dad's bed."

As Meg squealed, Hannah jumped up and clamped a hand over her mouth.

"Calm down! I didn't say he *would* die—I just said—"

"But he can't die!" Meg's voice was muffled, her face contorting in panic. "Jonathon said all his friend needs is to get warm and—"

"And you believe everything Jonathon says, right? Listen to me. That might not even be his real name—he could have just told us that. You *always* believe everything *anyone* says," Hannah said angrily. When Meg didn't reply, she bent down to look into her face. "If I let go, you promise you won't scream?"

Meg nodded. She took several deep breaths, then sat down carefully on the bed beside Hannah.

"Isn't there anyone we can call?" she whispered.

"The only way we can get help is to go after it ourselves," Hannah sighed. "And in this weather, that's impossible."

She leaned forward miserably and rested her elbows on her knees.

"What are the odds?" she groaned, and Meg gave her a funny look.

"What?"

"I mean, what are the odds of something like this happening to us, right here, right now?"

Meg was silent for a long while. Finally she stole a cautious look at Hannah.

"They don't look like escaped killers," she said quietly.

"Will you please stop with that escaped killer stuff? Murderers could look like anyone, Meg. They're shrewd and cunning and clever. *And* deadly."

"Well, anyway, the news said only *one* guy escaped."

"Oh. Only one. That certainly makes me feel better."

Hannah took a deep breath and lay back on the bed, staring up at the ceiling.

"Well, *I* don't think they look like escaped killers," Meg said again. "Did you really look at his face—the one on the floor, I mean?"

Hannah stared at her in surprise. "Did you?"

"Yes. He made me feel sad. I wanted to help him."

"Oh, that's just great." Hannah's voice rose, even though she tried to control it. "Him and every other stray who wanders into our yard! We're not talking about kittens or abandoned raccoons here, Meg, we're talking about—"

"I know, I know what we're talking about, but I don't know what to do either!" Meg's voice rose to match Hannah's. "I want to believe they're just guys in trouble, but I'm *scared*—I want to believe they're really nice and friendly and—and—"

"Harmless," Hannah murmured, and Meg gave a fierce nod.

"Yes! Harmless! But—oh, Hannah, I should have listened to you—I should never have let them in!"

"It wouldn't have done any good." Hannah relented

41

a little, seeing the stricken expression on Meg's face. "They would have broken in anyway, and then they might have been *really* mad."

Without warning Meg burst into tears. Hannah immediately grabbed her and tried to smother the sounds of her crying.

"Look at us," Hannah chided. *"Listen* to us! What are we doing to ourselves?"

For a few seconds Meg sobbed uncontrollably. And then, slowly, she pulled away and stared into Hannah's face.

"What?" she sniffled. "What are we doing?"

"This is crazy," Hannah mumbled, reaching for the tissues on the nightstand, handing one to Meg. "This is so crazy, all of this. I mean . . . we hear a stupid news report that has nothing at all to do with us, and then some poor guys just happen to have a wreck in the middle of a blizzard, and we're hiding here in our own house, scared to death they're going to kill us!"

Meg watched and said nothing.

"Coincidences." Hannah shook her head slowly. "A string of stupid coincidences, that's all. And we're letting our imaginations run away with us."

Meg considered this. She blew her nose loudly into the tissue and wiped one hand across her eyes.

"If we were them," she said quietly, "how would *we* feel if the people helping us thought we were escaped killers?" She paused, then gave a solemn nod. "That would really hurt my feelings."

The laugh popped out before Hannah could stop it. She clapped her hand over her mouth and wondered for one second if she might really be on the verge of hysterics. *It's nothing. . . . You're supposed to be tak-*

*ing care of things, and all you're doing is scaring Meg to death. . . . If Kurt hadn't called and threatened you, you wouldn't be nearly so paranoid—*

"Jonathon's too nice to be crazy," Meg said softly, and Hannah jolted back to the present.

"What?"

"You're trying to convince yourself everything's okay, but I can tell you're still worried, aren't you?" Meg frowned slightly. "Well, think about this— Jonathon's in there taking care of his friend. And he *did* offer to go somewhere else so you and I wouldn't be scared."

"Sometimes crazy people can seem just as normal as anyone else," Hannah murmured before she could stop herself. *Like Kurt always seemed so perfect.* "And just as nice as anyone else." *Like Kurt was always so wonderful when things were going his way—*

"Well . . ." Meg thought a moment. "Neither one of those guys seems crazy to me."

Hannah sighed and got up, pacing slowly back and forth between the bed and the closet.

"Meg, one of them hasn't done anything but lie on the floor since he got here. We don't know what's wrong with him—we don't even know how either of them got hurt."

"Yes, we do. They said they went off a bridge."

"Right. They *said*."

*This is crazy! I can't believe I'm actually standing here having this conversation with Meg. I can't believe we're actually alone in the house with two total strangers who are right across the hall in Mom and Dad's bedroom.*

Biting her lip, Hannah walked over to the window

and folded her arms on the sill. Beyond the glass, the night whirled by, a blinding kaleidoscope of black and snowy white. She closed her eyes and rubbed her aching forehead.

"Okay, you're right, they didn't actually do anything threatening," she agreed at last. After another pause she added almost reluctantly, "Actually, Jonathon just seemed really tired. And shaken up."

"And really worried about his friend. Wouldn't you be?"

Hannah let Meg's words sink in. She remembered the deep blue wells of Jonathon's eyes. She glanced toward the bedroom door and then back again to the window.

"Hannah," Meg said hopefully, "you know . . . we probably really are just scaring ourselves, don't you think? They're probably just two nice, normal guys . . . don't you think?"

*And if they're not just two nice, normal guys, then who are they?* Hannah's breath clouded the pane, and she ran her hand slowly across the glass. *If they're not just two nice, normal guys, and if you and I don't act nice and normal while they're here, aren't they going to wonder why we're scared of them?*

Hannah's gaze settled back on the window, on the millions of tiny snowflakes whirling through the sky, just like the millions of questions and doubts and arguments whirling through her brain. She wished she'd never heard that stupid news report. She wished she and Meg could just run from the house and go somewhere safe. She wished her parents were home . . . wished the phone would ring . . . wished she'd never broken up with Kurt, wished he'd never said those horrible things to her, wished he were here right now to protect her and make those guys go away, wished there'd never ever been a knock at the front door—

"You're right," she heard herself say, and she could feel a fake smile forming on her lips. "They're in trouble, and we've got to help. We wouldn't want them to think we suspect them of anything."

"That'd be rude," Meg agreed, climbing into bed. She snuggled down beside Bruce, who was already snoring. "Hannah?"

"Hmmm?"

"You're always so sensible about things. If you weren't here, I'd probably be freaking out. But thanks to you, now I feel just fine."

Hannah didn't answer. She leaned her forehead against the glass and welcomed the icy shock against her skin.

"Anyway," Meg murmured drowsily, "deranged killers only escape in the movies, right?"

"Go to sleep," Hannah said.

"Aren't you coming?"

"In a minute. I want to get Mom's radio so I can hear the weather."

"Here's a flash for you," Meg giggled, burrowing deeper beneath the blankets. "It's snowing."

It didn't take long for Meg to fall asleep. In less than ten minutes Hannah heard the deep, slow rhythm of her sister's breathing, and then she carefully slipped out into the hall.

Jonathon obviously wasn't sleeping in Meg's room. As Hannah stood there in the dark, she looked through the open door next to hers and saw Meg's empty bed. A sliver of light showed beneath her parents' door across the hall, so she tiptoed over, put her ear to the wood, and listened.

Silence.

After several long moments, she lifted her hand to knock . . . hesitated . . . then tapped softly.

Still no sound.

Holding her breath, Hannah inched the door open and stood for a moment, staring.

The bedside lamp cast eerie shadows over one small section of the room. She could see the covers lumped narrowly in the center of the bed, and in a chair alongside, Jonathon was sleeping, long legs stretched out, a blanket half covering his chest. He was still in his same clothes, and Hannah could see a dark stain on the rug beneath one foot.

She stood there, trying to decide what to do.

At last she crossed the room, pulled the blanket from the floor, and very slowly leaned toward Jonathon to cover him.

The shadow was swift and silent.

It flowed out from the wall so smoothly that at first all she felt was the crush of fingers against her throat and the merciless strength of a body pressed warm and hard against her back.

"Don't move."

The voice was deep . . . dangerous . . . and as it whispered against her ear, shivers raced wildly down Hannah's spine. She gasped and tried to scream, but the arm around her neck only squeezed tighter, and she could smell mud and wet hair and damp skin—

"One sound," the voice mumbled. "And you won't even know you're dead."

# 6

"Let her go!"

Through a haze of terror Hannah heard Jonathon cry out—saw him jump from the chair and start toward her.

"Stop it, Lance! What the hell do you think you're doing!"

The pressure around her neck let up. Someone pushed her from behind, and Hannah stumbled forward into Jonathon's arms.

"What's the matter with you—are you crazy!"

Jonathon sounded furious. As Hannah tried to pull free, he made a quick inspection of her neck, then thrust her firmly aside. In the pale lamplight he looked like a ghost, and a fine sheen of sweat covered his forehead and upper lip.

"Jon—" she began, but he moved away from her, his eyes locked on a shadow near the bedroom door.

"This is her house!" Jonathon exclaimed. "If it weren't for her, we'd still be out there in the—"

His words choked off. With a confused glance at Hannah, he swayed and fell heavily against the end of the bed.

For one split second Hannah stood there frozen. She wanted to run—to grab Meg—to get out of the house and away from Lance—but as she looked down at Jonathon, she couldn't seem to move.

And again she sensed rather than saw the movement behind her—so noiseless, so incredibly fast, that she scarcely even realized what was happening— only saw the arms reaching out for Jonathon and lowering him back into the chair.

"It's his leg," the deep voice said, and as the shadowy figure turned to face her, Hannah recognized Jonathon's companion. Long black hair fell damply to his bare shoulders. Muddy jeans hugged low on his narrow hips, and through the gloom, his coal-black eyes held her in a relentless, almost accusing stare. "Why didn't you help him?"

Hannah stared at him, dazed. "I tried, but—"

"It's not her fault," Jonathon said, but Lance didn't seem to hear. There was the sound of ripping cloth as he tore Jonathon's pants the rest of the way up his thigh.

"I *tried* to help him," Hannah started again, "but he wouldn't let me. I didn't know how bad it was—I—"

"I'm fine," Jonathon insisted weakly.

"Get something to clean him up." Lance shot a dark look in Hannah's direction, then muttered, "God, just look at this mess."

Hannah looked. Then she ran into the bathroom and leaned over the sink, trying not to be sick.

48

"Hurry!" Lance's voice cut through the silence, and she automatically began gathering washcloths and alcohol and a roll of gauze. *What am I doing—I must be crazy—he tried to kill me—* She found a small pan under the sink and filled it with warm water, then she took a deep breath and carried everything back into the bedroom.

Something had sliced jaggedly through the side of Jonathon's leg. From midcalf to midthigh, Hannah could see a gaping chasm of mangled flesh and dried blood, with something white showing through that looked suspiciously like bone.

"Strong stomach?" Lance asked.

"Wh-What?" Hannah looked up, startled. For an endless moment he held her gaze, then smoothly shifted his attention back to Jonathon's leg.

"I said . . . do you have a strong stomach?" Lance repeated. "Or would you like to leave the room again?"

Everything was all mixed up. Hannah could see him working on Jonathon's wound, and she swallowed hard, fighting for control. At last she raised her chin and gave him a defiant stare. "I'm not going to faint, if that's what you mean."

"So glad to hear it," Lance murmured. "Hand me that cloth."

As Jonathon watched Lance soak the rag in alcohol, Hannah could swear he went three shades paler.

"Like to hold on to something?" Lance asked casually.

He lowered the rag toward Jonathon's leg, and without thinking, Hannah grabbed hold of Jonathon's hand. She saw the split second of surprise on his face, and then the wave of agony as the alcohol made contact and his whole body went rigid. To Hannah's amazement, he didn't utter a sound . . . only one faint, sharp gasp as he turned his head away into the back of the chair.

"Okay?" Lance mumbled.

Hannah saw Jonathon nod.

"Stay with me, then. I know what I'm doing."

Hannah couldn't watch. Jonathon was squeezing her so tightly, she couldn't feel any sensation in her hand anymore. She concentrated instead on the side view of his face against the cushions . . . delicate features almost, not the sharp, chiseled angles of Lance—and yet there was a firm set to his chin and jaw, and a stubbornness to his mouth, and the lingering trace of a deep summer tan—

"—stitches," Lance was saying, and as Hannah snapped back to attention, she saw Jonathon shake his head.

"No," he murmured. "No stitches."

"You should," Lance added, shrugging, "after what happened to you."

"What *did* happen to him?" Hannah asked, glancing from Lance's determined face to Jonathon's pale one. "Was it from the wreck?"

Lance threw her a puzzled glance. "Wreck?"

"The wreck," Jonathon mumbled. "When my car went off the bridge."

Again he stiffened in the chair; again Lance pushed him down.

"He doesn't remember," Jonathon told Hannah. He paused and drew a deep breath. "He . . . he was unconscious when I pulled him out—he doesn't remember—"

50

'Shut up," Lance said. "Don't try to talk."

"He's so pale," Hannah worried. "Should he be that pale?"

Jonathon's mouth moved in a wry smile. *"I'm* not going to faint either. So you don't have to talk about me like I'm not here."

"Wreck, huh?" Lance murmured, and his eyes flicked briefly to Jonathon's face. "So *that's* what happened."

"He didn't mean it," Jonathon went on, looking back at Hannah. "Just now when you came in—" For an instant his hand tightened on her arm, and he gritted his teeth in pain. "He didn't know. He doesn't remember everything . . . or . . . how I got him here. He probably thought—"

"That someone was breaking in," Lance finished calmly, not looking up. His long slender fingers worked deftly. His dark hair fell forward, hiding his face. "That you were going to do something to Jonathon. Yes, he's right, I was confused. I couldn't figure out where I was."

"So you attacked me," Hannah said, her voice tight with anger.

"Attacked?" From the indifference in his voice, Lance might just as well have been discussing the weather. "If I'd really attacked you, you'd be hurt now, right? But you're obviously *not* hurt, so that obviously was no attack."

Hannah was furious. For the moment her fear was entirely forgotten.

"Don't you ever do that again," she seethed. "If you do, I'll—"

She broke off as Lance looked up. His eyes

narrowed slowly and held her in a long, discomfiting stare.

"I get the message," he said at last. "Hand me that other cloth, will you?"

Hannah threw it at him. Lance took it without a word and went back to his work.

"Well, Jonathon," he said quietly, "what have you gotten us into?"

Jonathon said nothing, only laid his head back and closed his eyes. Hannah watched as Lance finished securing the bandage on Jonathon's leg, then she took the pan of bloody water into the bathroom. Emptying it into the sink, she stood and stared at her reflection in the mirror. She seemed almost ghostlike somehow, as strange and unreal as everything that was happening tonight. She couldn't think clearly. She couldn't seem to focus. She ran cold water and splashed it over her face, rubbing her cheeks briskly with a towel, grinding the terry cloth into her skin. *Radio,* she remembered suddenly—*I've got to get Mom's radio.*

She put her ear against the bathroom door. From the other side she could hear the soft exchange of voices, but couldn't make out what they were saying. She thought of Meg sleeping, of how totally useless Bruce was, and she quickly turned the knob and started out.

Around her the house gave a huge groan.

The walls seemed to breathe and shudder; the windows rattled violently in their frames.

As the lights went out, Hannah froze in the bathroom doorway, her heart exploding in her chest. She heard vague movements in the darkness, and then the reassurance of Jonathon's voice.

"Are you there?" he called out. "Don't be afraid."

"Why should she be afraid?" Lance sounded almost amused. "She's got us here to protect her."

Hannah followed the direction of his voice. She could just make out his silhouette against the window-pane, and she moved carefully, cautiously, toward the hall.

"I'll get some flashlights," she said, and her hand brushed lightly along the surface of her parents' dresser, searching for the radio that was always there. A good radio . . . one with batteries . . . the only one in the whole house they could ever use when the electricity went out . . .

"Maybe I should go with you," Jonathon said, but her fingers had found it now, closed around its compact size and tucked it into the pocket of her robe, and she was moving out through the door, pulling it shut behind her.

"No," she said quickly, and then again, more firmly this time, "No, really, you should rest, and I'll find some lanterns or candles or something. You'll both feel better if you get some sleep."

If they answered, she didn't hear. She hurried to her room in the dark, and she slammed and locked the door, and then she sat on the edge of her bed and grabbed a flashlight from her nightstand drawer and pulled the radio out of her pocket and switched it on.

Nothing happened.

Puzzled, Hannah began rotating the dial—back and forth—back and forth—searching for signals, static, anything, but hearing only silence.

"It's got to work," she mumbled, "it's got to, Meg was playing it just yesterday, this doesn't make sense!"

And then she was rummaging through her desk, trying to find something to loosen the screws, and her head was pounding, pounding as she finally pulled the screws free and popped the back panel off the radio

Hannah shone her flashlight into the tiny compartment.

She stared down at it, and then she lowered the radio slowly into her lap.

The batteries were gone.

# 7

"Is it still snowing?"

Meg sat up and rubbed her eyes, squinting at the bedroom window. Beside her Bruce gave a congested snort and promptly rolled over on his side for forty more winks.

Hannah grunted from the closet doorway. She zipped up her jeans and pulled a sweatshirt down over her wool sweater.

"It slowed down for a while, but it's starting up again," she mumbled.

"How do you know—did you stay up all night?"

Hannah avoided the question. "Electricity's out, too."

"You're kidding! When did that happen?"

"Last night," Hannah said. "When you were asleep."

"Well, just look at us." Meg grinned at her. "Here

we are—neither one of us murdered in our beds. Guess those guys weren't killers after all!"

Hannah held her tongue and inched open the door to the hall. After listening several minutes, she glanced back at her sister and motioned toward the stairs.

"I'm going down. Keep the door locked till you're dressed and everything, understand?"

"Yes, Mother."

"I mean it."

"Yes, Mother."

Hannah glared at her. "Did you take the batteries out of Mom's radio?"

Meg looked blank. "No. Why would I do that?"

"I just wondered, that's all."

"Doesn't it work? I was just using it yesterday. I know I didn't break it." She stopped and wrinkled her brow. "Did I? Did I break it?"

Hannah sighed and shook her head. "Come down as soon as you can. Don't hang around in here."

"Are you going to check on those guys? To see if they're all right?" Meg thought a moment, and then her eyes widened in alarm. "Maybe they're *not* all right! Maybe that one guy died! Or maybe they're both gone! Maybe they left in the middle of the night . . . as mysteriously as they came—"

Hannah closed the door, cutting Meg off midsentence. Bruce had squeezed out beside her at the last second, and as she hesitated in front of her parents' room, he sniffed anxiously along the floorboards. Hannah nudged him down the hall and hurried downstairs.

The house was freezing cold. Frowning, Hannah

checked the thermostat and saw that it had dropped ten degrees.

"No," she sighed, leaning her head against the wall. "Don't go out on me now . . . please. . . ."

She didn't know the first thing about furnaces. She knew theirs was somewhere in the basement, but that was all. Moving the switch to a warmer setting, she waited to hear the heat come on, but nothing happened. *Maybe it's just overworked, maybe it's just resting and it'll come back on again in a little while. . . .*

She went into the kitchen. She knew Dad always kept a few kerosene heaters stored in the garage for emergencies, but she had no idea where they were. She was almost afraid to turn on the water, for fear the pipes had frozen up, but to her relief, it came out in a sputtering stream. *And the stove's gas, so at least we can cook.*

Hannah wiped her hands on a dish towel and opened the pantry door. Maybe things weren't so bad after all. She'd been so tired last night, so worried about Mom and Dad, so irritated with Meg, so upset about Kurt. When those two guys showed up, she'd jumped to conclusions and let her imagination run away with her. *That's not like me. . . . Meg's right . . . I'm always so sensible.*

"Escaped killers," she mumbled to herself, and actually laughed out loud. "God, what was I thinking?"

If she and Meg were really lucky, maybe the power would be back on again in twenty-four hours—but deep down, Hannah knew that was pushing it. The realtor had warned them about storms like these, warned them that this house was always one of the last to get electricity. What else was it she'd told them? The last time there'd been a blizzard, it had taken almost a week to get the power restored. . . .

*I've got to find some batteries.*

Hannah began hunting through drawers and cabinets. To her frustration, there seemed to be every other kind of junk in the world except batteries. *This is crazy. . . . We must have some somewhere. . . .*

She slammed the last drawer shut and stood there, frowning. It was so cold in here, she was starting to shiver. Heading for the back door, Hannah was shocked to see her breath clouding in the air, and there seemed to be a draft swirling somewhere around her ankles. Reaching for the dead bolt, her hand stopped in midair.

The door wasn't even locked.

In fact, it was standing open about two inches, and a cold blast of air was hissing in across the floor.

*I know I locked the door last night.*

Her mind did a quick flashback. She remembered checking every door and window before she'd gone to bed. . . . She was positive she'd checked this door, too. . . .

*Didn't I?*

Hannah flung it open, fighting down a wave of panic. The early morning world lay before her, still and endlessly white, camouflaged in perfect swells of snow.

*Maybe I only thought I locked the door. It's possible it could have stuck. . . . It's possible the wind could have worked it open during the night. . . .*

Her eyes fell to the clean sweep of porch, but there wasn't a trace of footprints. She couldn't even tell

anymore where the back porch left off and the yard
began—buildings, trees, shrubs, and fence posts were
now just so many shapeless blurs—and as snowflakes
fell faster from the leaden sky, Hannah felt her heart
sink within her.

*We'll never be able to get away from here now.*

With the closest neighbors miles away and the roads
impassable, there was no way they could go anywhere
for help.

*And no way those guys can leave either . . .*

"Bruce, get away from there," Hannah scolded,
hearing the telltale scratching of paws against wood.
As usual, he was crouched down in front of the
storeroom door with his nose to the crack, whining
softly. Hannah sighed and crouched beside him, shaking a finger in his comical face.

"Mice, Bruce. Understand? Yucky."

Bruce cocked his head and seemed to be contem-
plating these words of wisdom.

"Mice," Hannah said again. She knocked on the
storeroom door, and Bruce promptly barked. "Dad
hasn't patched all the holes in there yet, so the mice
can get in. And that's as far as we want them to go.
Got it?"

"I don't know. I'm not sure it's quite sinking in."

Hannah whirled with a cry. She hadn't heard anyone come into the kitchen, but now as the voice spoke
behind her, she saw Jonathon framed in the doorway
to the hall.

"What are you doing here?" she burst out, jumping
up again. Bruce gave a congenial woof and slipped out
the back door as Hannah reached over to pull it shut.

"What am I doing here?" Jonathon repeated. "At
the moment, not very much."

"Where's your friend?"

For a moment he didn't answer. His eyes stayed calmly upon her face, and at last he shook his head.

"Upstairs, I guess—"

"You guess? Don't you know?"

"Your sister's safe," Jonathon said quietly, "if that's what you mean."

Hannah flushed. Squaring her shoulders, she crossed to the counter and began filling the teakettle with water.

"I'm sorry," Jonathon sighed. "I know after what he did last night, you have every right to feel—"

"A little paranoid? A tiny bit threatened?"

"He'd just been in a wreck. He'd hurt his head and he was confused. *He* probably felt threatened."

A dark image of Lance loomed in Hannah's mind. She couldn't conceive of him feeling threatened by anything.

"Forget it," Hannah muttered. *Stay calm. Stay nice. They'll be gone soon.* "It wasn't your fault. I understand, he's your friend."

"Well . . . he . . ." Jonathon hesitated, searching for words. "He's not actually my friend—"

"What?"

"Well, what I mean," Jonathon said uncomfortably, "is that I only met him last night."

Hannah stared back at him over her shoulder. He looked tired and strained, and there were dark smudges beneath his eyes.

"You . . . don't even know this guy?" Hannah fixed him with an incredulous stare. "But I thought—"

"Look, I had a wreck, and he was hurt, and I tried to help him." Jonathon paused, helplessly spreading his hands. "It wasn't like we were properly introduced."

Hannah's stomach churned. She gripped the edge of the counter and tried to stay calm.

"I don't know what to say," Jonathon offered at last. "I couldn't just leave him there—he might have died. What was I supposed to do? If it hadn't been for you and your sister . . ." His voice trailed off. Hannah heard him sigh. "I don't even know your name," he said.

Hannah didn't answer. She stared down at the thin curl of steam rising from the teakettle on the stove. She held one hand above it, relishing its warmth.

"I wish you'd just go," she said at last. "I wish both of you would just leave."

"We are," Jonathon replied, and once more Hannah turned to look at him. "That's why I came down," he went on quietly. "To tell you that . . . and to thank you."

An unexpected ache went through her. Jonathon wasn't standing quite straight, she could see that now—he was propped against the wall, taking his weight on his good leg. He was still wearing the same muddy clothes, and his ragged jeans hung open around his bandage.

"You . . ." Her eyes darted to the kitchen window, to the falling snow beyond. *Good . . . it's what you wanted, isn't it—let him go . . . let them both go . . .* "You really think you can walk on that leg?"

Jonathon smiled. "I think I'll have to."

But Hannah couldn't look away now. She stared at his bandage, then lifted her eyes reluctantly to his face. His cheeks looked a little more sunken . . . a little more pale than they had last night. A thought passed vaguely through her mind that he might actually have lost a lot of blood. . . .

"Well . . ." With difficulty Hannah forced her attention back to the stove. She wiped her hands on a dish towel and noticed they were shaking. *You've got to think of Meg—you know they can't stay here—*

"My name's Hannah," she said abruptly.

*Why did I do that? I must be out of my mind. Don't say anything to him . . . don't volunteer anything—*

She turned off the burner and took the teakettle off. She got two mugs from the cupboard.

"Where will you go?" she burst out, before she could stop herself.

"There must be another house around here—" he began, but Hannah cut him off.

"Not for at least three miles. And the roads . . ." *Stop it—what are you doing, are you insane—let them go!* "And all those hills and woods and . . ."

She trailed off, gazing helplessly out the window. Then she looked back over her shoulder and took a long, determined breath.

"There must be something around here that'll fit you—some of my brother's old things maybe, if Dad's are too big. You can't go outside in those pants, you'll freeze to death. And I could fix some sandwiches. You could take them with you."

Jonathon regarded her in silence. He pushed himself away from the doorframe and took a tentative step into the hall.

"No, thanks. You've done enough already."

"But—"

Hannah bit her lip, watching as he disappeared. *I had to do it—I couldn't let them stay—Jonathon's right, I've done plenty for them already—much, much more than some people would. . . .*

She leaned on the counter and buried her face in her

hands. After a while she heard Meg's familiar skip down the stairs, and then a muffled blend of voices. *What's taking them so long—why don't they leave!* Hannah followed the sounds to the living room, where she stopped in dismay.

Jonathon was in the chair by the front window, one hand slowly stroking Bruce, who was shaking snow all over the rug. Lance was leaning over the hearth, tossing logs into the fireplace. A blaze was already roaring up the chimney, and as he pulled back to rub his hands together, Meg shyly handed him the poker.

"There's an escaped killer loose around here somewhere," she was saying. "We heard about it on TV."

Hannah felt like she'd been punched. She opened her mouth to yell, but Meg was chattering on.

"He killed some guards and then he stole a woman's car, and then he killed the woman."

"Meg," Hannah mumbled, but Meg didn't answer, and Hannah suddenly realized they hadn't noticed her yet standing there just inside the door. She saw a strange look cross Jonathon's face . . . saw him turn his head in slow motion and look directly at Lance. For just the briefest moment Lance returned the gaze, but then his eyes shifted to Meg's face . . . lingered there . . . finally slid back to the flames.

"Is that so?" Lance said calmly. "I'd like to hear about it."

"Well, we don't really know anything," Meg sighed. "Hannah tried to watch it on TV, but she fell asleep."

Now Jonathon was staring at Meg, too. As Hannah watched him, he suddenly ducked his head as though something on the floor were extremely fascinating, and then he turned his attention to the window.

"But they must have said something about him."

Jonathon's tone was just as casual. "Something you remember."

Meg thought hard for a moment, then shrugged. "Only that he's dangerous. And that if anyone sees him, they shouldn't take chances—just call the police. Oh—I remember now—he *strangled* those guards. That's how he got out."

Meg sounded so pleased with herself. As Bruce butted up against her, she smiled and buried her face in his furry neck. Hannah felt her own stomach sink lower and lower.

"So . . ." Lance's nod was almost imperceptible. "You don't even know what he looks like. This escaped killer."

Meg shook her head. "They said he might be headed this way, but I bet he's probably in another state by now. He wouldn't come here."

Lance stared into the fire. "And what makes you think that?" he murmured.

"Well . . . because of where we are. So far away from everything. How would he ever find us?"

The silence stretched on and on. Hannah heard the soft crackle of logs . . . the hiss of falling ash. . . .

"We found you," Lance said.

"Meg." Hannah's voice sounded unnaturally loud. "Would you come here, please?"

She turned and started for the door. Without warning, hands clamped down on her shoulders, and as she spun around in fear, she saw Lance's narrowed eyes gazing down at her.

"I think this changes things a little," he said solemnly.

Hannah winced and tried to pull away. "What— what do you mean? Changes *what* things? How—"

"We couldn't possibly leave now," Lance murmured, and Jonathon was moving across the room, too, joining Lance beside the door, nodding his head in slow concern.

"Not leave?" Hannah stammered. "But—but—you just said—" She took a step back, but Jonathon's arm was across the threshold behind her and she couldn't get past—

"I agree with Lance," Jonathon broke in. "You girls are stranded out here."

For just a second Lance's grip tightened on Hannah's shoulders. His eyes locked with Jonathon's in a long, unreadable stare.

"It just wouldn't be right to leave you two alone," Jonathon murmured.

"How lucky we found your house last night," Lance added softly. "It must have been fate."

**8**

"Why did you *tell* them that!"

Hannah was so furious, she could hardly get the words out. Meg sat at the foot of the bed, her eyes wide and scared.

"And what were you doing alone in there with Lance?" Hannah ranted on. "I told you to hurry up and come down where I was—"

"You did not. You said not to hang around in the bedroom. And *you* were alone in the kitchen with Jonathon, so why is that any different?" Meg's voice rose defensively. "And anyway, Lance went down to check the furnace—it's a disaster, he said—and then he went out and brought in some wood and got the fire going so the house would warm up! He was only helping!"

"*We* could have gotten the fire going—we don't need his help," Hannah threw back. She paced the width of the bedroom, her hands knotted into fists at her sides. "I can't believe you told them about that killer—I just can't believe it! What on earth ever possessed you!"

"Well . . ." Meg's lower lip trembled, and she wrapped her arms tight around her chest. "Well . . . I don't know . . . it just came out when I wasn't thinking. And I don't know why you're so upset about it. They're being nice enough to stay and—"

"But they *weren't* going to stay, don't you understand?" Hannah stomped her foot. "That's the whole point! I'd just talked them into leaving!"

"Leaving?" Meg echoed, her face blank. "In this weather? You were going to make them leave?"

Hannah turned away, gnawing her bottom lip. It wouldn't do any good to shout at Meg—it would only make her cry.

"I can't believe you were going to turn them out in all this snow," Meg went on, clearly dumbfounded. "With both of them hurt? If Mom and Dad were here, they'd *never* do that—"

"Well, if Mom and Dad were here, we wouldn't be having all these problems now, would we?" Hannah snapped.

Meg's mouth clamped shut. Her eyes filled with tears, and she threw herself across the bed. Hannah opened her mouth to say more, thought better of it, then stormed out, slamming the door behind her. She heard Meg lock it from the other side.

Jonathon and Lance were still in the living room. They were standing beside the fireplace deep in conversation, and Hannah purposely ignored them as she hurried to the kitchen. Grabbing her jacket from the back of a chair, she went out to the porch and allowed herself the satisfaction of slamming another door.

*Oh, God, what am I going to do?*

She knew it was all up to her, just like everything was *always* up to her because Meg was totally useless. Hannah had always been the one in charge, the one to get things done; she'd never had the soft feelings that Meg had, the easily swayed emotions, the stupid trust that Meg always put in people. *The wrong people,* Hannah thought grimly. *Escaped killers . . . psychopaths . . . those kinds of people . . .*

She started down the steps and promptly plunged into three feet of snow.

Sputtering, arms flailing, Hannah floundered for several minutes before finally managing a foothold. Heaving herself up again, she grabbed the edge of the porch and inched sideways until she could stand straight. She surveyed the white, unbroken expanse of lawn and wondered for one crazy minute if she might actually be dreaming this whole thing—that maybe by pinching herself hard enough, she'd wake up and find herself in bed, and hear Mom and Dad downstairs at breakfast, and have the joy of discovering that someone had kidnapped Meg in the middle of the night and she'd never have to see her again.

"No such luck," Hannah grumbled. Sighing deeply, she maneuvered around the drifts that had piled against the porch, and finally managed to find a walkable route to the garage. Guys or no guys, she still had to keep the house warm, which meant finding those stupid heaters.

The wind was sharp and raw, stinging her cheeks a bright red. She could feel her feet freezing up, and she chided herself for not having taken the time to put on snow boots. All she'd thought about was getting away—from Meg, from those—

Those—

*Those what?*

Hannah stopped and shook her head in amazement.

The whole idea was suddenly so bizarre and incredible that she wanted to laugh.

*Psychopaths . . . murderers . . . escaped killers . . .*

"The truth is, Hannah Stuart, you have absolutely no idea *who* those two guys are, standing back there in your living room," she groaned. She hesitated, thinking of Meg, anger and worry struggling within her. *She'll be okay . . . she has her door locked. . . .* She trudged on through the snow, talking out loud to herself in her sternest tone of voice. "That escaped killer idea *is* pretty far-fetched, you have to admit. I mean, if one of them was a murderer, he'd have killed us all by now, right? Right."

*But last night Lance did try to kill me—just like that crazy killer strangled those guards to escape—*

"No, he didn't," Hannah scolded herself again. "He was just confused from that bump on his head. He's no escaped killer." She made herself say it again, louder this time. "He's *no* escaped killer. But that still doesn't mean he's not crazy. Or dangerous."

She stopped abruptly, put her gloves to her lips, and blew fiercely on her cold hands.

*Listen to yourself. You're starting to sound like Meg.*

Hannah lowered her hands and thrust them deep in her pockets. There were knots in her stomach, and she

69

took a long, deep gulp of cold air. *But no matter who those guys are, we still have to be careful. Whoever they are, Meg and I are still alone with them—and if we act too suspicious and scared, that could be dangerous . . . and if we act too nice and trusting, that could be dangerous, too.*

"Heaters, Hannah," she said to herself through clenched teeth. "Heaters, remember? Deal with one thing at a time."

She looked back over her shoulder, eyes focusing on her bedroom window. With a twinge of guilt, she wondered if Meg was still up there crying. She should never have left Meg alone . . . she should have made her come out and help, gotten her away from those two scary guys in the living room.

Squinting her eyes, Hannah tried to peer through the falling snow, tried to see off into the cold, gray distance.

"I'm doing the best I can," she whispered fiercely to herself. "I can't force them to leave, can I? I'm doing the only thing I can do."

She had to find those heaters. If she didn't, the house would be unbearable by tonight.

She plowed ahead, hunching her shoulders against the wind. The familiar backyard was an alien place today, everything distorted and disfigured by snow. The old work shed . . . the lawn chairs . . . the barbecue . . . It dawned on her suddenly how very much like oversized headstones they all looked, leaning and crouching and lurching through some huge abandoned graveyard. She tried to go faster, her breath burning in her lungs, and at last she was even with the woodpile. She barely even glanced at it as

70

she passed, but then suddenly she stopped and frowned.

*Something's different.*

Hannah backed up. Slowly her eyes swept over the huge pile of wood . . . the snowy contour of the tree stump beside it . . . the scatterings of dead leaves and pine needles sticking up through the uneven drifts. Something had been through here recently, she noticed—trampling down the snow, breaking through its smooth crust. Whatever it was had cut a wide, irregular swath the whole length of the wood-pile.

Hannah leaned over to examine it more closely. There were no footprints, yet the snow had definitely been disturbed. It had that slightly fuzzy appearance as though something had stirred it up, then tried to smooth it back again. . . . *Like something's been dragged . . .*

Bewildered, she followed the trail with her eyes, trying to shake off her eerie feeling. It wasn't unusual to find impressions like this when the wind and snow were blowing so hard—drifts could change and re-arrange themselves, tracks could come and go and grow three times their original size. *So what are you stopping for?*

Hannah straightened up again. She was close to the driveway now, and the garage was only a short walk away. Chiding herself for being so jumpy, she started off again, stopping short when she heard something behind her.

"Who's there!"

Hannah spun around. She squinted her eyes against the cold, and she stared.

A log had dislodged from the top of the stack . . . rolled off the woodpile . . . landed on the ground.

The snow fell faster now.

Everything was still.

*Normal . . . normal . . .*

And yet it *wasn't* normal—she could *feel* it— a nagging insistence gnawing at the corners of her mind.

Again her gaze went slowly over the woodpile . . . the tree stump . . . the log half-buried in the snow.

*Something's wrong. . . .*

*But what?*

She clenched her hands in her pockets.

She glanced back nervously over her shoulder . . . off to her right side . . . her left. . . .

She started to turn away when she suddenly noticed something at the edge of the woodpile, very close to where she was standing. In that particular spot some of the logs overlapped and formed a sort of overhang, shielding one small section of ground from the drifts piled high around it.

Hannah looked down into the snowy niche.

What she saw there was dark and splotchy . . . sprayed out across the pure, clean white. . . .

Her heart caught in her chest. She moved slowly forward, closer and closer.

And she could see it much better now—the thick red stain . . . the thick red globs spattered over the ground—yet even now they were fading . . . fading . . . beneath a fresh new swirl of snow. . . .

Hannah turned and ran.

She ran without stopping, her cries ragged in her throat, and when she finally got close to the porch, she stumbled and fell, struggling up again, her eyes wildly searching the back of the house.

She saw her window on the second floor—the face peering out, half-hidden by curtains.

But it wasn't Meg looking down at her from the bedroom.

It was Lance.

"Meg!" Hannah shouted. "Where are you?"

The house was quiet. As Hannah slammed the back door, Bruce jumped away from the storeroom and guiltily dropped something at Hannah's feet.

Hannah looked down at the dead mouse and shuddered.

"Get that thing away from me! *Meg!*" In growing panic Hannah kicked at the mouse and shoved Bruce aside. She ran for the hall, jumping back with a scream as she collided with Lance in the doorway.

"Looking for your sister?" he asked, and Hannah froze, her heart leaping into her throat.

"Where is she?" Hannah demanded. "Where's Meg?" She tried to step around him, but he moved sideways at the same time. To her fury, she found herself trapped between Lance and the wall.

Hannah looked up at him, fighting back panic.

She could see the gash across his forehead, washed

74

clean now and practically hidden by his hair. To her surprise, there were other smaller cuts on his face that she hadn't noticed before. A dark stubble was starting to show across his chin and upper lip. His eyes held hers in a hard stare.

"If you don't let me go," Hannah threatened, "I'll—"

"No one's holding you," Lance said. He lifted his arms at his sides, and Hannah suddenly realized that he'd backed away. Flushing angrily, she shoved past him and ran up to her room.

"Meg!" she shouted. "Meg, where are you?"

"She's in the basement," Lance said, and Hannah whirled around. He was standing behind her in the doorway. She hadn't even heard him coming.

"She's . . . where?" Hannah echoed weakly.

"In the basement. Getting something from the freezer, I think she said." Lance folded his arms across his chest. "All that panic for nothing."

Hannah didn't answer him. She walked over to the window and leaned back against the sill. She waited till she was sure her voice wouldn't quiver.

"What were you doing in my room a few minutes ago?" she finally asked.

"I wasn't in your room."

"Don't lie to me—I saw you when I was outside!"

"Then you must have made a mistake. What possible reason would I have for being in your room?"

Hannah took an angry step toward him. From the floor below came the sudden sound of a door closing, and then feet rushing up the stairs. To Hannah's relief, she saw Meg out in the hallway, but as Lance moved aside to let her through, Meg stopped and stared at the two of them.

75

"I need to talk to you." Hannah motioned her sister to come in, but Meg stayed where she was.

"Why?" she demanded stiffly. "What have I done now?"

"Do you *mind?*" Hannah said to Lance. She marched over, pulled Meg inside, and slammed the door in Lance's face. Then she turned back to where Meg was sitting on the bed. "Meg, listen to me."

"I'm listening. What is it?"

"There's something out there by the woodpile."

"What . . . kind of something?" Meg asked suspiciously.

"It . . ." Hannah crossed to the window and looked out. She could see the woodpile in the far corner of the yard—the snow-covered logs . . . the shapeless tree stump . . . *but something's still not right. . . . What is it?* "It looks like blood," she finished, and Meg gave a high-pitched squeal.

"Blood! Oh, Hannah, did Bruce kill something?"

This time it was Hannah's turn to stare. She watched as Meg covered her face with her hands and gave a little moan.

"What was it?" Meg wailed. "Did you see it? No, don't tell me—you'll have to bury it, Hannah, you know I can't stand to look at it! Maybe Lance or Jonathon can bury it! This is so awful! Bruce never catches anything anymore—he's so slow, and he can't see a thing—"

But Hannah only heard the first few words of Meg's babbling. She leaned heavily against the wall, a dull throbbing through her brain, and she pressed her hands to her temples.

*Bruce. Of course. How could I be so stupid . . . ?*

"An animal," Hannah murmured, and Meg sniffled and wiped her eyes with one sleeve.

"Did you see it, Hannah? Was it a squirrel or a rabbit? He must have done it when he went out this morning. Oh, I can't stand it, I can't even think about it. Why did you tell me?"

Hannah stared at her. *A squirrel . . . a rabbit?* But Meg was right—Bruce hadn't been able to catch animals for a long time now. Not being so blind and deaf and lame . . .

"Hannah?" Meg persisted, and before she thought, Hannah mumbled, "I don't know what it was. I didn't see it."

"So we can't bury it?"

Hannah shook her head.

"Do you think he brought it inside?" Meg jumped up in alarm. "Do you think it's somewhere in the house?"

"I . . ." She remembered the mouse Bruce had presented her downstairs. *No . . . whatever this was, it was much too messy for a mouse.* "I don't know. I hope not."

"Let's tell the guys. Maybe they'll be able to find it." Meg stood up and started for the door, then stopped and gave Hannah a quizzical look. "Are you all right?"

"What?" Hannah mumbled. *No, obviously I'm not all right or I wouldn't have assumed—what? Whatever horrible thing I was assuming.* She laughed at herself, a silent laugh with no humor in it at all. *Just an animal . . . What was I thinking?*

"But there weren't any pawprints." She frowned. "Even with Bruce's big feet . . ."

77

Meg stared back, her face brightening. "Then maybe it wasn't Bruce who killed it after all. Maybe it was some other—you know—predator. A coyote or a fox or a . . . a stray cat or . . . I don't know . . . something. And the snow already covered everything up."

Of course that could happen—hadn't she already thought of that earlier with the snow blowing down around her and the wind shifting back and forth? And yet still Hannah looked doubtful. "Maybe. I guess."

Before she even knew what was happening, Meg threw both arms around her, hugging her tight.

"Poor Hannah—that really upset you, didn't it? You always act so brave and strong, but you felt bad for that little animal, didn't you? It's okay, Hannah— it's just that all these horrible things keep happening. You breaking up with Kurt, and then Lance and Jonathon showing up. But really, I think they're okay—or at least Jonathon is. I've been talking to him, and he seems really nice. I'm not sure about that Lance guy, though. He stares a lot. I don't think he likes to talk much."

Hannah disentangled herself from Meg's arms. "Stop it—I'm perfectly fine."

"No, you're not. But it'll all work out." Meg smiled confidently. "You'll see."

Before Hannah could answer, Meg opened the door, then jumped back with a gasp.

"Oh, Jonathon! You scared me!"

Startled, Hannah came up behind Meg. Jonathon was in the hall, backing away from the threshold and looking very embarrassed.

"Uh . . . sorry. I was just . . ."

He recovered himself and gave them a sheepish smile. But Hannah had caught the quick look he threw past them into the bedroom, and she also caught the quick shadowy movement just past his shoulder. A second later Lance, too, appeared in the hall behind him.

"Just looking for . . . gloves," Jonathon finished, shrugging his shoulders apologetically. His eyes were back on Meg now, and Meg was nodding at him and smiling. "I just came up here looking for gloves. We thought we'd carry in some more wood and . . . well, do you have any extra?"

"We're not out of wood yet, are we?" Hannah asked, and *You're a bad liar, Jonathon,* she wanted to tell him, but instead she kept quiet and met his gaze levelly. *Just how long have you been listening at the door?*

"In the front closet," Meg said. "Come on. I'll show you."

"Thanks."

Jonathon gave Hannah a quick smile, which she didn't return. Meg went downstairs, but instead of following, Jonathon and Lance stood there in the hall.

"Is that your boyfriend?" Jonathon asked.

Hannah looked at him in surprise. Her fingers tightened on the doorframe, and she tried to keep her voice steady.

"My boyfriend? What do you mean?"

"The picture." Jonathon pointed to the framed photograph on the nightstand by her bed. "That guy you're with. Is he your boyfriend?"

*He used to be. . . . Right now I wish he were.*

Hannah kept her eyes on Jonathon. "Yes. And he's coming over today."

Lance seemed to be studying the photo. It had been taken last summer at the beach, and Hannah was in the foreground wearing Kurt's baseball cap, and Kurt was standing a little ways behind her, tanned and gorgeous in his swim trunks, mugging at the camera. She saw Lance frown slightly.

"What's wrong?" she demanded.

"Nothing. It's just that . . ." He shook his head. "I couldn't know him. I'm not from around here."

Shrugging, he turned and went downstairs, leaving Jonathon and Hannah alone.

"He *is* coming over today," Hannah repeated emphatically. "And bringing some of his friends. They're all football players, and my boyfriend's extremely jealous."

Jonathon's gaze shifted from the picture to Hannah.

"Like the road crews? Look, Hannah, your boyfriend won't be coming today. You know it, and I know it. So why keep playing games?"

"What games? It's not a game—"

"Look, I understand why you're nervous about us being here, but what do I have to do to convince you we're not going to tie you up, rob your house, and have our way with you?"

Hannah flushed deeply. "That's not funny."

"No," Jonathon said solemnly. "It's *not* funny. So I wish you'd stop making me feel like a criminal. It could just as easily be the other way around, you know."

"How's that?"

"As a matter of fact, I should be just as suspicious of you. I don't know you; I don't even know if this is really your house. You and that girl down there you claim is your sister could have come in and murdered all the people who live here, and now you're impersonating them. It could happen."

Hannah glared at him. "Is that supposed to be funny?"

"Maybe you even have a dungeon downstairs where you keep unwary travelers who happen to skid off bridges."

"*I* didn't try to strangle you," she reminded him, and turned her back.

Jonathon didn't answer.

He closed the door softly behind him, and Hannah heard him go down the stairs.

She went back to the window and stared out.

She gazed down at the woodpile in the far corner of the yard . . . at the jagged pattern of footprints she'd made tracking through the snow.

Someone else was making tracks there now.

Lance.

Stiffening, Hannah pressed her nose against the windowpane. What was he doing out there—getting more firewood? But she and Meg had practically filled the porch with logs last night, so there was no reason for Lance to be going to the woodpile.

Puzzled, she stood and watched as he made his way across the yard, a black flowing shadow on white. His long legs gave him the appearance of gliding; his movements were easy and graceful. He paused at the woodpile and looked around, then knelt close to the spot Hannah had examined earlier. She saw him put his hand to the ground . . . saw him lift it close to his face. Then he got up, took the half-buried log from the ground, and began stirring up the little section of bloodied snow.

A cold lump of fear twisted in Hannah's stomach. As she kept watching, Lance stood back to inspect his work, then tossed the log onto the woodpile.

"Hannah?" Meg said.

Hannah nearly jumped out of her skin. "Will you quit sneaking up on me like that?" she snapped. "What do you want?"

"The heaters," Meg said, sounding hurt. "I thought you were going to get some heaters."

Hannah gave a vague nod. "Yes. The garage."

"I found hot dogs and stuff in the freezer," Meg went on. "I thought maybe we could roast them in the fireplace. We have lots left over from that family reunion, remember?"

"Great," Hannah mumbled. "A picnic. How cozy."

Meg gave a huge sigh and shook her head. "Hannah, you know, you *could* cheer up a little. It's not the end of the world. Come on! A picnic by the fire'll be fun!"

Hannah didn't answer. She turned her attention back to the window and watched as Lance headed for the house. His long hair billowed out around his shoulders, powdered thickly with snow.

"He's handsome, isn't he?" Meg murmured at her back.

Hannah whirled and fixed Meg with a withering look. "Don't even think about it, Meg. Stay away from him."

"All he needs is a long cape," Meg said. "And he'd look just like a knight or a pirate or something." She sighed deeply. "Jonathon, too, only something more sophisticated. An artist, maybe, or one of those nineteenth-century poets."

Hannah could feel herself panicking, but she forced calm into her voice. "I mean it, Meg. I know all those stupid romantic ideas you get in your head. You know you always end up getting hurt. And this *isn't* a fairy tale."

"All I said was, I think he's handsome—"

"I know what you said, and I know how you are," Hannah said sharply. "And the only reason you think Lance is so fascinating is because you're afraid of him."

"What's that supposed to mean!"

"It means . . . oh, I don't know what it means. Just forget it."

Hannah bit her lip, fighting for patience. She stared at Meg's downcast face and tried again.

"Look . . . I'm sorry. I just want this thing to be over, okay? I just want them to leave—"

"But maybe they won't leave!" Meg's voice rose even as Hannah tried to shush her. "Maybe they won't leave for a long, long time! We can't just go around being terrified the whole time they're here!"

Hannah looked at her helplessly, but Meg rushed on.

"We're *all* stuck here, Hannah—the least we can do is try to get along with each other. *They're* trying to cooperate. *You're* the one who's being a big pain in the butt."

With that, Meg stormed out of the room, leaving

Hannah openmouthed. She sank down onto the bed, trying to sort out her thoughts.

*Is it me?*

A mixture of half anger, half fear settled in the pit of her stomach. She stretched out across the covers, cradling her head on folded arms.

*So I'm being a pain in the butt. And all this time I thought I was protecting us.*

Her eyes wandered reluctantly to the nightstand, to the picture of her and Kurt at the beach. *Oh, Kurt, I wish you were here.* She wondered if he'd been able to make his ski trip this weekend after all . . . where he was right now . . . if he was thinking of her. His threats still echoed in her mind, and she fought back a sudden rush of tears. Of course he hadn't really meant what he said, he'd just been hurt and upset. After he'd had time to calm down, he'd forgive her. Maybe they could even still be friends. . . .

"Right," Hannah muttered to herself. "And you thought Meg had romantic ideals."

Restlessly she got up and crossed to the window, staring out at the wintry day. The snow was falling faster now—she could hardly even see the tracks anymore where Lance's footprints crisscrossed the yard.

*Meg's probably right,* she thought. *Bruce must have had himself quite a time, recapturing some of his youth, stalking some poor little animal that was half-frozen and too helpless to get away. . . .*

Once more her eyes swept over the far corner of the yard, and then slowly, slowly she straightened.

*That woodpile . . .*

That woodpile all lumpy and shapeless beneath its

thick coating of snow, with the broad, flat stump practically buried beside it and the drifts piled so high—

And suddenly she knew what was different about it . . . what was missing . . . what was so horribly wrong—

"The tree stump," Hannah murmured. "Where's the axe?"

# 10

"Where are you going?" Jonathon asked.

Hannah sat on the kitchen floor, wrestling with her snow boots. As Jonathon appeared in the doorway, she looked up at him with an annoyed frown.

"I've got to find some heaters in the garage," she said stiffly. "Do you mind?"

Wincing a little, he leaned over and took hold of the boot still dangling from her left foot. With one sharp tug, he pulled it easily into place.

"I'll help you," he said. His fingers closed around her elbow, lifting her to her feet, and before Hannah could protest, he was out the door onto the porch.

Hannah took a flashlight and followed, pausing a minute to study him as she shut the door. He was on the top step buttoning his jacket, his shoulders hunched against the wind, his hair tousled. Pain had etched itself into the tight lines of his cheeks, and he leaned a little to one side. Hannah noticed that he'd finally changed clothes, and though her dad's things hung a little too large on Jonathon's slender frame, the dark blue of his turtleneck set off the perfect blue of his eyes. Without warning he looked at her, giving her a quick strained smile. Hannah flushed and turned away.

"You shouldn't be out here," she said crossly. "You'll start bleeding again."

He smiled another faint smile. "Careful. You almost sound like you care."

"Well, I don't."

"I said almost."

Hannah pushed past him and plunged off the steps, floundering awkwardly through the drifts. She didn't care if he came with her or not—whether he fell or not. In fact, she wished he *would* fall, so she could just leave him there and the snow would cover him up forever.

"It doesn't look like it'll let up anytime soon," Jonathon observed, squinting up into the sky. "We could be stranded here for days."

Fear fluttered in Hannah's throat. After several swallows, she managed to choke it back down.

"I really don't need any help out here, okay?" she reminded him, but Jonathon didn't take the hint.

"That escaped killer," he said carefully. He was walking behind her, and Hannah realized she'd slowed her pace to match his own. "Do they really think he's around here?"

Hannah gave him a sharp glance. In spite of her gloves, she could feel sweat on the palms of her hands.

"I don't know. That was last night when I heard the report. I don't know what's happened since then."

Jonathon gave a vague nod. "It's strange, isn't it?" he murmured.

"What is?"

"This." His arms moved in an inclusive gesture, and he frowned. "I was thinking about what Lance said—about fate. We're all here together. . . . None of us really know each other."

Hannah didn't answer. Her foot caught unexpectedly on a buried tree root, and as she pitched forward, Jonathon reached out and caught her.

"You all right?" he asked, and Hannah jerked out of his grasp.

"I'm fine. I told you, I don't need any help."

"Yes, I can see that."

Hannah pushed ahead of him. He was limping badly, trying to keep up, and she deliberately went faster.

"What's with you?" Jonathon said breathlessly. "You on some kind of mission?"

"I told you, I have things to do."

She squinted off toward the woodpile. She could see the stacks of logs, the snowy heap of the tree stump. A blast of wind sent snow into her eyes and she put up her hand to shield her face.

"If it weren't for this stupid weather, Mom and Dad would be home by now," she muttered, and was surprised when Jonathon heard her.

"I'd be home by now, too," he said, "if I hadn't wrecked my car."

"You should have been driving more carefully," Hannah reminded him. "Then you wouldn't have had the wreck at all, and you wouldn't have hurt Lance, and none of this would ever have happened."

She felt wickedly smug about it. She glanced back at him struggling to keep up, and she kept on walking.

"You thought I *caused* the wreck?" Jonathon asked. "You thought *I* hurt Lance?"

He stopped then. He sounded so surprised that Hannah stopped, too, and faced him.

"I didn't *cause* the wreck," Jonathon said slowly. "I was just driving along, minding my own business. I came around a turn, and there was this bridge ahead of me, and this car was just stopped there sideways, rammed headfirst through the guardrail, blocking my lane. It must have hit some ice and skidded thirty feet at least, 'cause the railing was ripped away all down the side. I didn't have any warning at all. I tried to ease down on my brakes, but the pavement was like solid glass. That's when I felt my own car going off the bridge."

Hannah stared at him. He was looking down at the ground, and as the memory came back to him, he slowly shook his head.

"I don't remember the impact. But suddenly it was cold, and there was water around my legs. My door was open, and I started to crawl out—that's when I realized I was in a lake or something. The water was frozen, all these big chunks floating around, and I'd crashed through all this ice."

"Brewer's Pond," Hannah mumbled. For a brief instant she had an image of Jonathon being sucked beneath the frozen surface of the water. She shut her eyes and forced the image away.

"I managed to pull myself out," Jonathon went on. "I started back toward the incline, and that's when I realized I wasn't alone down there."

Hannah opened her eyes. A deep shiver went through her, much colder than the snow.

"Lance?" she gasped. "But . . . but how?"

"He was just lying there at the edge of the shore, right below the busted guardrail. My guess is, he got thrown from his car when it slammed into the railing."

"But he doesn't remember anything?"

Jonathon's answer was negative. "He was bleeding and soaking wet, and he'd hit his head. It's a miracle I even got him walking at all." His face darkened. "I was trying to pull him up the slope when all of a sudden I heard this noise. I think in the back of my mind, I must have known what it was. . . . I just couldn't believe it."

He stopped. He stared at Hannah for so long that she began to feel uneasy. She opened her mouth to prompt him, but at last he seemed to collect himself and went on.

"It was coming from above us . . . an engine revving and wheels spinning. I looked up at that car, and suddenly its headlights came on—they were so bright, they practically blinded me. That's when it dawned on me that someone *else* was in that car—that maybe Lance hadn't even been driving it. I yelled, but nobody answered. And by the time I dragged Lance up to the bridge again, the car was gone."

Hannah's mouth dropped open. "You're not serious. You're not telling me that whoever was in that wreck with Lance just drove off and left him there?"

"That's exactly what I'm telling you."

Hannah hugged her arms tightly around her chest. She was feeling colder by the second.

"I don't even know how I hurt my leg." Jonathon absently touched one hand to his thigh. "I didn't feel it happen. . . . I didn't even notice it till later."

Hannah peered at him through the falling snow. He looked drained and unhappy. He shook his head again and started walking.

Hannah hurried after him, placing her feet in the tracks of his boots.

"Didn't Lance tell you anything about him?" she asked. "The guy in the car?"

Jonathon shrugged. "I don't think Lance even knew him. He just hitched a ride with him."

"But why would the other guy just leave like that? Especially after they'd had a wreck?" Hannah thought a minute. "To get help, maybe?"

"I was there," Jonathon said dryly. "He obviously *knew* I was there when I took a dive into the pond."

"Maybe he panicked," Hannah mused. "Maybe he thought Lance was dead."

"Lance *looked* dead. And personally, I don't think the other guy cared."

"Maybe he was the escaped killer," Hannah said bluntly, and Jonathon threw her a startled glance.

"Well, he could have been," Hannah insisted.

That faint smile again. "Maybe so."

"I'm not trying to be funny about this," Hannah said irritably. "And you don't know anything about Lance. Maybe Lance had something to do with that car crashing. Maybe Lance grabbed the guy around the throat, and the guy crashed on purpose and ran for his life."

To Hannah's annoyance, Jonathon laughed. "I'd like to hear you tell Lance your theory."

"Well, don't you think it's a little strange?" Hannah retorted hotly. "That he'd be hitchhiking around here in this kind of weather?"

"He told me he'd been camping. He said the storm moved in so fast, all the access roads iced over before he could get out. He was trying to find shelter when the guy drove by and picked him up."

*Shelter—or a place to hide? And now he's in our house with Meg—*

"I'm sorry." Jonathon's smile faded. "I guess it's my fault you're so upset. I'm the one who brought Lance here in the first place." He shook his head, and Hannah could swear she heard him chuckle. "Escaped killer, huh?"

Hannah plowed past him, anger welling up in her throat. She crossed the last few feet to the woodpile, brushed fiercely at the tree stump, and stepped back in dismay.

"What's wrong?" Jonathon came up behind her "You look like you're going to cry."

"The axe is gone," Hannah murmured.

"What axe?"

"The axe that's always in that tree stump. The axe we always use to chop wood. The axe that should be there, only it's not!"

She started away from him, but he caught her arm.

"Come on, Hannah, it's not worth getting upset about. You've got plenty of firewood cut already—"

"But you don't understand—it was here before!' She yanked free, nearly losing her balance. Jonathon reached out for her again, but she managed to sidestep him.

"No," he said slowly, "I guess I don't understand."

Hannah stomped off, not caring if he followed or

not. As she reached the garage door, she slammed her fist against it and fought back frightened tears.

"You don't know *anything* about Lance!" she burst out again before she could help herself.

Jonathon stopped a safe distance behind her. His voice was very calm. "I don't think you need to worry about Lance."

"Just get away from me, okay?"

"You can't treat him like some criminal. You—"

"I don't want to talk about Lance anymore. Just drop it."

Finding a precarious foothold among the drifts, Hannah shoved at the garage door. When it popped open without warning, she felt her feet slide out from under her and pitched sideways into the snow, only to feel two arms go around her waist and yank her back.

Sputtering and twisting, Hannah found herself crushed up against Jonathon's chest. As she lifted her fists to swing at him, he pressed her even tighter against him, pinning her arms helplessly between their bodies.

"Let me go!" she shouted.

He was much stronger than he looked. As Hannah struggled harder, Jonathon's grip tightened. Her head was tilted back, and she looked straight up into the deep blue of his eyes.

"Please," she said breathlessly. "Let me go."

"If I do, you'll land right down there in the snow." A spark of amusement flickered in his eyes. Hannah tried to look away, but she couldn't turn her head.

"Let . . . me . . . go."

He was looking at her so intently, his eyes drawing her in, and she knew he must be able to feel the fierce pounding of her heart against his chest. A smile touched the corners of his mouth. Hannah felt herself blushing.

Jonathon's lips lightly touched her hair . . . her forehead. He kissed the tip of her nose.

"Jonathon . . ."

But his lips were on hers now, warm and soft and insistent, and as Hannah gasped and closed her eyes, a thousand sensations rushed through her, leaving her weak.

"You're shaking," Jonathon murmured. "Are you cold?"

He kissed her again. He kissed her lips, and then her chin, and then his kiss trailed slowly down her neck. Hannah felt like her whole body was on fire. She wanted to hit him—she wanted to cry—and she wanted—

"You want to get those heaters now?" Jonathon said softly. "I think . . . maybe . . . we better."

He stepped away from her. Struggling for composure, Hannah turned around and tried not to fall through the door.

"So where are these heaters?" Jonathon slapped his hands together, trying to warm them. "This place is like a meat locker."

"I know, it's terrible out here." Was that *her* voice trembling so hard? In a daze, Hannah snapped on the flashlight and began picking her way over boxes and cartons and piles of old junk. "You better stay there. You could hurt yourself."

"Thanks for the warning."

Grimacing a little, Jonathon lowered himself onto the front fender of the station wagon, then slowly let out his breath.

*"You* be careful," he told her. "I'm not sure I could carry you back to the house."

"I'm not sure I'd want you to."

To Hannah's surprise, she heard him chuckle.

"What's so funny?"

"You," Jonathon said.

"Why? What'd I do?"

"Absolutely nothing."

Hannah didn't know whether to laugh or be annoyed. Instead she worked her way along her father's workbench, rummaging through shelves and cabinets, pulling things out, stuffing them back in again.

"Maybe you should start your car," Jonathon said casually. "Just as long as we're out here."

Hannah kept on searching. "In case you haven't noticed, I don't think I could drive it very far."

"If your engine goes dead, you won't be able to drive it at all."

Distractedly Hannah felt in her coat pockets. "I don't have the keys with me."

"Where are they? I can come out and start it for you later."

"My purse maybe . . . and there's an extra set in the—"

Hannah caught herself in time. She slammed a wrench down on a shelf and heard Jonathon laugh softly.

"In case *you* haven't noticed, I don't think I could get very far either, even if I *was* a car thief."

Deliberately Hannah moved to another set of shelves, pretending she hadn't heard his remark.

"I don't know," she said at last, turning to him in frustration. "I know those heaters are here *somewhere.*"

"How many?"

"Four, I think. I don't know where Dad could have put them, but—"

She broke off as the garage walls gave a violent shudder. Wind shrieked softly through the cracks, and overhead the roof sagged and groaned.

"Uh . . . maybe we should get out of here," Jonathon suggested, but Hannah turned back to her task.

"It's okay," she assured him. "This garage is stronger than it looks. I hope."

"So do I."

Jonathon eased himself to his feet, and she could hear him moving off behind her, limping slowly across the concrete floor, picking things up, setting them back down.

"How old is this place, anyway?" he asked curiously.

"The garage—I'm not sure. But the house is over a hundred."

"I thought so. It's a great old place. Lots of character."

"And noises. It creaks and groans all the time. When we first moved in, Meg was positive we had hundreds of ghosts."

"And do you?"

Hannah frowned. "We could, I guess. I think some people died here."

For a moment there was silence. She heard a soft rustling sound, as though Jonathon might have shifted position. Then she heard him move through the shadows once more.

"Do you know what happened to them?" he asked.

Hannah paused a moment, trying to remember. "They were killed, I think. By someone in their family. Their son, maybe? But the realtor said it happened years ago."

Jonathon's voice floated softly back to her. "Lots of old houses probably have histories like that."

"My folks loved the idea of fixing the place up," Hannah went on. "And they've done a lot, but it takes such a long time. Like some of the rooms on the third floor are still shut off because there're holes in the walls, and the vents don't work, and the wiring's all screwed up."

"Well . . . I guess that's half the fun. Waiting to see how it'll all turn out."

Hannah continued her search. She heard Jonathon drop something and swear under his breath.

"Sure a lot of stuff in here," he said. "No wonder you're having so much trouble. If you really *did* want to hide something, no one would ever find it."

Hannah couldn't help smiling. "Meg hid a goat in here once."

"A goat?"

"She wanted to keep it for a pet, and Dad said no."

"Did she get away with it?"

"Not long. Goats aren't known for their wonderful aromas."

Jonathon laughed. "My kid brother's like that. Always getting in trouble."

"You have brothers and sisters?"

"Five. I'm the oldest."

Hannah glanced back at him over her shoulder. "So you were going home to see them this weekend?"

"I even skipped work yesterday to get an early start.

Thought I could beat the bad weather. Lot of good it did me."

Hannah watched as he inspected some old tires in a corner. "I'm sorry," she said at last.

"For what?" Jonathon straightened and regarded her in surprise. "If it hadn't been for you, Lance and I would be very frozen corpses by now."

Hannah turned away and resumed her search. "So . . . where do you work?"

Another long silence fell. Then Jonathon said, "Well, not in one place, exactly. I work construction, so . . . you know . . . it kind of changes from day to day."

"Construction?"

"Is that funny?"

"No," she said quickly, "I only meant . . ."

"What?"

"You don't . . . you know . . . *seem* like the construction type."

"And what *is* the construction type?"

"Nothing. I didn't mean—"

"Tattoos and big muscles? Careful, Hannah, this limp might be deceiving."

Hannah flushed with embarrassment. The memory of his strength was all too fresh in her mind, and she quickly changed the subject.

"Where do you live?" she asked.

"In a trailer. What is this, a census?"

"I mean, what town do you live in?"

"I told you," Jonathon replied, his voice casual. "I move around a lot. Hey, I think I just found your heaters."

Hannah maneuvered her way back to him, where he

stood pointing up at the ceiling. Wedged in tightly among the rafters were the objects of her search, and she threw Jonathon a grateful smile.

"Thanks. Now, how do we get them down?"

"No problem. I'll just jump for them."

His lips moved in that hint of a smile, and Hannah couldn't help but smile back.

"There's got to be a ladder out here somewhere," she said. "Now, if I can just find it."

Beside her Jonathon picked up a broom and began poking between the open beams.

"Maybe we can knock them down. I can stand on one of those boxes."

"No, don't. You'll hurt yourself."

"They're really crammed in," Jonathon muttered. "I don't know how your dad ever got them up there in the first place."

"You hold the flashlight. Let me have the broom."

Jonathon took one last stab at the ceiling. In the pale glow of the flashlight, his face looked ghostly, and Hannah chided herself for not having noticed before now.

"Let's just go back to the house," she said. "Maybe Lance can get the heaters—you should be lying down."

"I'm okay."

"You're white as a sheet," Hannah argued. "You've been on that leg long enough."

"I'm just . . . dizzy." His expression was half-embarrassed, half-disgusted. "Sorry. Just give me a second."

"Here. Sit down."

Hannah reached for him, but his body reeled slowly

99

in the opposite direction. As he took a clumsy step to keep from falling, she scanned the clutter around them, trying to find a clear spot on the floor to lower him down.

"Maybe you're right," Jonathon mumbled.

Hannah grabbed his arm, and he leaned heavily against her. She wondered what she'd do if he passed out.

Jonathon nodded toward the opposite end of the garage. "How about the car . . . ?"

"Great idea."

Immediately Hannah steered him toward the station wagon, half dragging him over piles of junk. She glanced down at his leg and saw fresh blood seeping through his jeans.

"Oh, Jonathon, you're bleeding again."

"Sorry." He managed a weak smile. "I'll try to do better next time."

They reached the car at last. Hannah started to open the back door, but it was locked. She propped Jonathon against the side of the car.

"Stay right there."

"Don't worry."

"If you'd listened to me in the first place, this wouldn't have happened."

Jonathon tried to look contrite.

Yanking open the passenger door, Hannah automatically reached for the lock control. And then as her eyes swept over the seat, she felt herself slowly freeze.

Something was lying there in a bloody heap, tangled and slashed to ribbons.

It took her several seconds to realize that the thing had once been a sweater . . . and that it was hers.

"My God . . ." Hannah murmured, and in spite of

her horror, she reached out and carefully lifted the edge of one sleeve.

Something rolled out of it.

Something even more bloody and mangled than the sweater.

With a shriek, Hannah jumped back as the glazed eyes of the rat stared up at her.

"What is it—what's wrong?"

Hannah spun around, right into Jonathon. As his arm went around her, she pressed her face to him, her voice muffled against his chest.

"It's Kurt!"

*"What?"* Jonathon leaned closer, trying to hear.

"That's my sweater! Kurt's been here!"

"Kurt? Who's Kurt?"

"My boyfriend."

Suddenly aware of their position, Hannah pulled away, making a valiant effort to compose herself. Jonathon peered over the top of her head and let out a long, low whistle.

*"Your* sweater?"

"I left it in his car when we went out last weekend."

"Hmmm . . . had something else to keep you warm, I guess."

"Actually, I don't think that's any of your business."

Jonathon leaned back against the car. He moved his hands down his leg, carefully avoiding the wound, and took note of Hannah's indignant expression.

"Sorry. When you screamed just now, I was sure something had upset you."

Hannah stared at him. He clenched his jaw . . . drew a sharp breath . . . gingerly shifted his weight.

"I—I *was* upset," she relented. "A little."

Jonathon said nothing.

Several seconds dragged by, and finally Hannah burst out, "No, I'm *very* upset! Don't you understand —this means he's *been* here! He's been here, and for all I know, he could *still* be here!"

The garage door flew open, and they both jumped. Without hesitation Jonathon stepped in front of Hannah, then let out his breath when Lance entered the garage.

"You've been gone a long time," Lance said. "We were getting worried."

Before Hannah could stop him, Jonathon nodded at the station wagon. "Take a look at this."

"What?"

"It's nothing—" Hannah insisted, but Lance was already walking over. She tried to close the car door, and Jonathon held it open.

"She says her boyfriend did it," Jonathon said.

Lance leaned forward to stare at the front seat. Hannah saw his shoulders tighten . . . saw his finger gently prod the cold, stiff rat. Jonathon made a face and looked away.

"Your . . . boyfriend," Lance echoed, shooting Hannah a sharp glance. "As a joke?"

Hannah paused, then miserably shook her head.

"Nice guy," Lance muttered.

"You don't understand," Hannah insisted, feeling suddenly that she had to defend Kurt against these total strangers. "See . . . we had a fight, and I broke up with him. He's just mad, but he'll get over it. I mean, he has this terrible temper, but he's just *mad* now and—"

"How mad?" Jonathon asked softly, and Hannah stared at him.

"What?"

"How . . . mad?"

She felt trapped. She felt like the walls of the garage were closing in on her. She wrapped her arms around herself and bit down hard on her bottom lip.

"He . . ." Somehow she managed to choke out the words. "He threatened to . . . kill me."

Lance raised an eyebrow, exchanging silent looks with Jonathon.

"Kill you," he repeated, as though somehow the message weren't quite getting through. "You broke up with him, and so now, to get even, he's going to kill you."

"Look, I know it sounds crazy—"

"No," Jonathon broke in, "*he* sounds crazy. Is this the guy up there in the picture?"

Hannah nodded.

"And you think he came out in this snowstorm," Jonathon went on, "all the way out here in this blizzard, just to leave this in your car?"

"I was going to use the car," Hannah tried to explain. "He knew I was going to pick up my parents at the airport last night. He even said something about the road I'd be taking, how he knew it'd be dark and deserted—"

"So your parents aren't even in town?" Lance's eyes narrowed, and Hannah felt panic building in her chest.

"They *should* be here—they were *supposed* to be here—only they're snowed in—"

"Calm down." Jonathon put a hand on her shoulder. "Lance and I are here, and anyway, you're probably right. Your boyfriend's just playing a joke on you and—"

"It's not a joke," Lance broke in. "Anyone who goes around killing animals isn't trying to be funny."

Jonathon glanced reluctantly into the car once more.

"It's a warning," Lance insisted. "He's trying to scare her."

"He's very jealous," Hannah tried to tell them. "He accused me of seeing someone else—"

"Well, are you?" Jonathon asked.

"Am I what?"

"Seeing someone else. Is some other guy just suddenly going to show up here out of the blue?"

"No, of course not. I'm not seeing anyone else—"

"If it *is* him, he could be watching the house right now," Lance said matter-of-factly.

"I'm sure he wouldn't try to hurt me." Hannah sounded desperate, even to herself. "He probably just wanted to scare me a little—not really terrorize me or anything."

"Fear *is* terrorizing," Lance said. He reached into the car and rolled the rat up in the sliced remains of Hannah's sweater. "Some people really get off on fear."

"He's right, you know." Jonathon gave a grim smile and carefully shifted position. "They use fear instead of guns or knives. Fear's the most powerful weapon there is."

Hannah glared at them. "Thanks. Both of you. You're making me feel a whole lot better."

"If he *is* still out there," Lance said again, "then that means he's probably been watching the house all along. Which opens up a whole new set of problems."

Hannah glanced at Jonathon. He was trying so hard to appear normal, but he could barely stand up.

"Can we just go inside?" Hannah cut Lance off. "I think Jonathon needs to lie down and—"

"If he *has* been watching the house," Lance went on coolly, "then he knows Jonathon and I are here with you."

The implication hung there between them in the cold, cold air.

"You mean—" Hannah swallowed tightly. "You mean . . . Kurt might think that you or Jonathon and I are—"

"Lance is right," Jonathon murmured. "And if your boyfriend's as jealous as you say he is . . . who knows what he might do next."

# 12

"Don't say anything about this to Meg, okay?" Hannah pleaded as the three of them came back into the kitchen.

Lance nodded and set the kerosene heaters down on the floor. Jonathon sank into a chair, not even resisting when Lance knelt beside him and inspected the bloody fabric of his jeans.

"It's going to keep doing that," Lance said, frowning. "Unless you let me stitch it up."

Jonathon shook his head. "No. It'll stop in a minute. If I sit down for a while—"

"It won't stop. You're losing too much blood. Each time you use it, you're making it worse."

Jonathon glanced over at Hannah. Now that she could see him clearly again, she was alarmed at how pale he'd grown.

"You can't do that," Hannah protested, as Lance

stood up again. "You can't just sew him up like he's a—a—rag doll or something! You're not even a doctor!"

"I've worked in hospitals," Lance said calmly. "Get me a needle and thread and some alcohol. And clean—"

"But what if he dies? You could kill him!"

Lance fixed her with an unblinking stare. "And what if infection sets in? And what if he loses that leg?"

Jonathon looked positively ashen. As Hannah stood there in desperation, he finally nodded at her.

"He's right. You'd better do it."

"I can help," said a timid voice behind them, and they all turned to see Meg standing in the doorway.

"Don't be ridiculous." Hannah scowled at her. "You can't even stand to get a splinter."

For a long moment Lance stared at Meg. Hannah had the weirdest feeling that he actually almost smiled.

"Go on, Meg, get out of here," Hannah ordered. "If you want to help, get some washcloths and more gauze and tape."

"I'm worried about Bruce. I can't find him anywhere."

"Well, go worry about him in the other room."

"I mean it. I haven't seen him for hours."

Hannah put her hands on her hips, patience wearing thin. "Check all the closets."

"I already have."

"The basement, then."

"He's not anywhere."

"Well, we saw him this morning," Hannah recalled. "Has anyone seen him since then?"

"Maybe something's happened to him!" Meg insisted.

"Meg," Hannah said carefully, trying to avoid a panic situation, "you remember that animal we were talking about before? I bet Bruce went off somewhere to hide it. He's always going off to bury things—he'll be back."

"But what if he's lost? In all that snow?"

"He's not lost!" Hannah snapped before she could stop herself. "And we don't have time to stand here talking right now, okay?"

She marched over and took Meg's arm and led her firmly down the hall.

"But it's so cold out there!" Meg went on. "And it's cold in *here,* too. Can't you fix the heater?"

"No," Hannah said sharply. "Listen to me, Meg. Things are tense enough around here right now, and you're not helping."

"Are you really going to let Lance sew him up?" Meg asked.

Hannah put her hands on Meg's shoulders and backed her to the wall. "How can I stop him? If Jonathon agrees to do it, what can I say? All I know is, Jonathon's in agony right now, and he needs help, and there's no one else around here who can do anything for him."

"I had this feeling all along that Lance was wonderful."

"You did not." Hannah leaned down in Meg's face, her voice lowering. "And stop looking at Lance like that, Meg. I can see right through you."

"I don't know what you're talking about—"

"You most certainly do. For some reason that's totally beyond me, you're infatuated with him—"

"You don't know anything about what I am." Meg drew herself up indignantly. "And *you're* the one who was out in the garage with Jonathon for so long."

Hannah took a deep breath, measuring out every word. "Only—because—I—couldn't—find—the heaters."

"Well, it sure seemed to me you could have found them a whole lot sooner."

"And it sure seems to me you have some really empty spaces in that brain of yours. . . ."

Meg went upstairs in a huff, leaving Hannah to pull herself together. Jonathon—Lance—Kurt—Meg—and now Bruce, too. What else could possibly happen? She leaned her head against the wall, then jumped as a hand closed over her arm.

Lance stood there looking down at her. The sleeves of his shirt were rolled above his elbows, and Hannah could see the fine, hard ridges of veins along his arms.

"Living room okay?" he asked. "Jonathon shouldn't be climbing stairs."

Hannah managed a nod. "Yes. Fine. There's a bathroom off the hall near the front door." She thought a minute, then added, "I'll get some sheets and blankets. There're some extra in Meg's room."

"Perfect. Now all we need is something good and strong to numb his pain."

Hannah's heart sank. "My parents don't keep liquor in the house. Can't you think of something else?"

"Yeah. A strong blow to the head."

While Lance returned to the kitchen, Hannah went in search of her mother's sewing kit. When she came back down, Jonathon was lying on the couch in the living room, staring up at the ceiling.

"I feel stupid," he said flatly, and in spite of herself, Hannah laughed.

"If I were you, I'd feel scared instead."

"Thanks a lot. Just the support I need."

Quickly Hannah glanced around the room and out toward the hall.

*Where is he?* she mouthed. When Jonathon shrugged, she sat down on the edge of the couch beside him. "I mean, you can't ever hear him coming, he's so quiet."

"I think it's called stealth," Jonathon corrected her.

Hannah nodded. She wanted to say something, to make him feel better, but felt hopelessly at a loss.

"The point is," Jonathon said, as if he were reading her mind, "I don't have much choice, do I? You don't have to be a doctor to tell I'm in bad shape."

Hannah forced a smile. "It'll be fine."

"He *said* he's worked in a hospital," Jonathon reminded her.

Again Hannah nodded. She clasped her hands together and stared down at her fingers.

"The point is," Jonathon tried again, "I can hardly stand up, it hurts so bad. So—"

"I told you not to come with me to the garage!" Hannah burst out. "I told you not to walk on that leg—I could tell it was bothering you—"

"Uh-oh. Now you sound like you *really* almost care."

Hannah looked away. She could hear the teakettle whistling in the kitchen. She could hear Meg's feet creaking the floorboards overhead.

"You should never have come with me," she mumbled again. To her surprise, she felt his fingers close around her hand . . . squeeze gently. His touch was ice-cold.

"With that show in your station wagon?" He smiled. "I wouldn't have missed it for the world." When she didn't answer, Jonathon squeezed her hand harder. "Hey, Lance is a camper, right?"

"So he says."

"Right. So I figure he knows how to survive in the wild. And that means he has to know what to do if he's wounded. And *that* means—"

"Who are you trying to convince—me or you?"

Hannah got up and left the room. She met Lance coming out of the kitchen, but he passed her with barely a glance. He looked as casual as any fisherman getting ready to clean the day's catch.

*This is unbelievable—I'm in a nightmare—*

She didn't want to think about what was going on right now in the living room. She stood in the middle of the floor, eyes moving slowly between the windowpane and her jacket hanging on the back of a chair. She thought about the station wagon and her sweater and the dead rat stuffed inside. She didn't want to believe Kurt had done something so hideous—yet who else could it have been? Had it happened last night before the full brunt of the storm? Suppose he'd been watching the house all that time, just waiting for a chance to sneak in and do something worse—but before he'd been able to, Lance and Jonathon had shown up. . . .

"No," Hannah muttered to herself. "That's crazy."

*But no crazier than a bloody sweater and a dead rat . . .*

Maybe he'd spent hours out there, waiting. Watching. Had he hidden in his car? Sat there singing along with his stupid radio and planning his revenge? Or maybe the garage. Any footprints would have been covered up long ago. Or how about the woods? There were several sheds out past the tree line that Dad kept in good repair—sheds for storing tools and potting plants and keeping more junk that couldn't fit in the garage anymore.

*Or maybe he left the sweater and took off again, and right now he's miles away on his stupid ski trip, laughing his stupid head off every time he thinks about the shock I got when I opened the car door.*

Suddenly Hannah was angry. It was just like Kurt to be so juvenile about everything—to try and get back at her with grade-school pranks. He was probably gloating to his buddies even now, about how powerful he was and how scared he'd made her feel.

What was it Jonathon had said—about fear being the most powerful weapon?

"I'm going to fix those hot dogs," Meg announced, coming into the kitchen.

Startled, Hannah turned to stare at her. "Now?"

"Sure. I'm hungry, aren't you?"

Hannah sighed. One thing about Meg was that she never held a grudge for very long—or even remembered why she'd been mad. She watched as her sister went to the counter, gathered up bundles of hot dogs, then turned with a frown.

"Did you eat one of these?"

"Did I?" Hannah sounded puzzled. "You mean, did I eat a whole package by myself?"

"Well, one package is missing."

"No, I haven't touched your hot dogs. Maybe you counted wrong."

Meg counted again. "No . . . I'm sure I brought up three packages."

"Meg, that's thirty hot dogs. There're only four of us."

"And Bruce."

"Well, there's your answer. Bruce probably took a package and ate it."

"But I haven't seen him since then." The panicky tone crept into her voice, and Hannah tried to distract her.

"Don't forget the ketchup and mustard and stuff. But you'll have to wait awhile to cook those. Lance is in there working on Jonathon's leg."

Meg shuddered and sat down at the table. "You were right."

"About what?"

"About me not being able to help. I couldn't have watched it. And I hope he doesn't try to show me his stitches when it's over."

"I don't think you have to worry about that."

Hannah boosted herself up onto the countertop. She sat there looking at Meg, swinging her legs against the bottom cupboards.

"So," she sighed. "Here we are."

"Weird, huh?" Meg said, and Hannah gave a nod.

"Like something in a story that never happens in real life."

"Or a movie, where you don't know what's going to happen next, only we don't have background music to give it away."

Hannah nodded again. "I like that. That was good."

For a moment Meg savored the compliment. Then she said in a small voice, "Hannah?"

"What?"

"I've decided I don't really know what to think about either one of those guys."

Hannah shook her head. "I don't either, Meg."

"Really?"

"Really."

"But I still think they're cute," Meg said emphatically. "Both of them are really cute."

"How can you even think about that at a time like this?"

"Are you still worried about them?"

*I'm worried about everything. I'm worried about things you haven't even thought of to worry about.* "Of course I am. I've been worrying so much, my brain's numb."

"I guess there's only one thing we know for sure."

"What's that?"

"We're trapped."

Hannah gazed at Meg. It surprised her that she wasn't actually feeling fear or panic at the moment . . . just a weird sort of resignation.

"Do you hear anything from the living room?" she finally asked.

Meg shook her head and automatically covered her ears. "No, and I don't want to. You think he'll cry?"

"I don't know. I probably would."

"Think he'll be hungry?"

"Probably not for a while."

"We should be giving him something, shouldn't we?" Meg fretted. "For all the blood he's lost? Liver or something healthy like that?"

Before Hannah could answer, Lance came into the room. He was carrying a pan and washrags, and as he held them out to her, she saw they'd already been rinsed.

"He's got to stay quiet," Lance said, before they could even ask how Jonathon was. He squirted dishwashing liquid over his hands and started washing at the sink. "And if you have anything for pain, he's going to need lots of it."

"I'm going to look for Bruce," Meg said.

Lance shut off the water and reached for a towel. He dried his hands slowly, keeping one eye on Meg as she got into her coat and headed outside. Only when she'd finally closed the door behind her did he turn to Hannah.

"Does she know about this thing with your boyfriend?" he asked.

"Only that we broke up," Hannah said. "Not about the garage. I didn't want to scare her. Why?"

Lance looked down at the towel. His voice was very quiet. "She didn't sleep in her room last night, did she?"

"No . . ." Hannah's look went quickly from surprise to suspicion. "She slept with me. Why?"

"I think you better come see for yourself."

Terror seized her, even before she got to Meg's bedroom . . . even before she followed Lance inside.

At first everything seemed normal.

The canopy bed . . . the stuffed animal collection . . . the posters and banners and photos slapped all over the walls. Hannah stood and took everything in, and then she turned to Lance in bewilderment.

"I don't see—"

But she did see, then. She saw Lance's eyes fixed on Meg's bed, where the covers were tumbled and something lay in the very middle of the soft down comforter . . .

Something old and safe and familiar . . . something that made Hannah back away with a scream—

Meg's favorite teddy bear.

With an icepick through its heart.

# 13

*This is crazy . . . this is impossible—*

As Hannah staggered back, she felt Lance's hand close tightly around her arm, steadying her.

"How—how could this—" she stammered, but his fingers slid away, and he moved across to the window.

"Does your boyfriend know which room is Meg's?" he asked.

"Of course he does. He's been to the house lots of times."

"No chance he could have mixed it up with yours?"

Hannah shook her head.

"Not even from outside?"

"What's that supposed to mean?"

"Nothing. Unless he managed somehow to climb in the window when no one was around."

Hannah's heart raced. "That's impossible. One of us has been in the house all the time—haven't we?"

"But not upstairs," Lance reminded her. "And we don't know when this happened."

"But Meg got dressed this morning—she would have noticed it then."

"No. Not until she pulled her blanket down."

Hannah stared at him. "You mean—"

"A little surprise for Meg—under the covers." His lips tightened into a humorless smile. "Could be that Kurt will try to get to you through Meg."

It was too much to absorb; she couldn't take it all in. Hannah sank down on the window seat and put her hands to her head.

"What were you doing in here?" she asked softly.

"Looking for the extra sheets and blankets you told me about." He paused, then added, "Saving you the trouble."

Hannah stared at the floor. "But how did you find—"

"I was borrowing that blanket"—Lance jerked his chin in the direction of Meg's bed—"since I didn't see extra of anything lying around."

Hannah shifted her eyes to the teddy bear. "He's her favorite," she said sadly.

"Did he know that?"

"I don't know. It wouldn't have been hard to figure out, since she keeps him on the bed most of the time anyway." Angrily Hannah got to her feet. "It couldn't have been Kurt—how did he get in?"

Lance gazed out the window, down into the backyard below.

"Does he have a key?"

Hannah shuddered. "He could," she said miserably. She caught the sharp look Lance threw her and added, "He used mine once when we went out of town, so he could come by and check on the house. He could have had an extra one made before he gave it back to me."

"Well . . . he could have broken in," Lance murmured. He leaned closer to the window, examining the roofline below. *"Or* he could have climbed. You've got trees close to the house—gables like stepping-stones—even the top of the porch. It wouldn't be that hard for someone to come up. And with all this wind and snow, they wouldn't even leave prints."

"But . . ." Hannah was at a total loss. *"When?* And *how,* without us hearing? It's like . . . like he knew when the room would be empty."

For a moment there was silence. And when Lance finally spoke, his words chilled Hannah to her very soul.

"Maybe not. Maybe he thought Meg would be here."

They both turned as the back door slammed from downstairs. Hannah started toward the teddy bear, hesitated, then forced herself to pick it up.

"Give it to me." With one twist Lance pulled the icepick free. Bits of stuffing exploded softly around his fingertips.

"I'll think of something," Hannah said shakily, tucking the bear under her arm. "If I tell her Bruce got ahold of it, she'll be a lot less hysterical."

She hurried next door and tossed the bear into her closet. By the time she got back to Meg's room, Lance had straightened the bed and was standing by the window once more.

"Hey, where is everyone?" Meg stopped in the hall

and peeked in at them, her expression bewildered. "What's going on?"

"We're . . ."—quickly Hannah opened a drawer and pulled out a stack of bed linens—"uh . . . just getting these sheets and blankets. Jonathon's going to be sleeping downstairs."

"Okay," Meg agreed. "Is anyone hungry?"

Hannah had never felt less like eating. "Sure. Go ahead and fix the hot dogs, why don't you."

"I'll take these," Lance said, and Hannah surrendered the sheets and pillowcases without a word, watching as he and Meg disappeared together down the stairs.

*"Maybe he thought Meg would be here. . . ."*

Hannah felt cold all the way through. She glanced around nervously, half expecting Kurt to suddenly spring out at her from some hidden panel in the bedroom wall. *So is he going to hurt me by trying to hurt Meg?*

Her mind did a rapid series of flashbacks, trying to recall everything that had happened since yesterday. *Yesterday?* Was it only twenty-four hours ago that she and Meg had been coming home from school and life was so routine?

Since that time all of them—she and Meg and Jonathon and Lance—*all* of them had been upstairs at one time or another. Any of them could have slipped into Meg's room. . . .

*And I know I saw Lance looking out of my bedroom window this morning, even though he denies it. . . .*

Hannah frowned and went out into the hall. *"Fear's the most powerful weapon there is. . . ."*

Would Kurt go this far to get back at her? Unhappily, Hannah had to admit he would. However he'd managed to do it, this definitely had his trademark of sick humor.

She wandered into the kitchen. She felt like a robot programmed for normalcy. *I have to get through this. . . . I can't let Meg know anything's wrong. . . .*

"Still upset about Kurt?" Meg looked up from the sink as Hannah went past her. For one weird second Hannah stared back at her, totally thrown.

"What are you talking about?"

Meg shrugged. "You know. The breakup. You have that look on your face you always get when he upsets you."

Hannah was feeling sicker by the minute. "Do I? No, it's not Kurt. It's . . ."

She couldn't think of anything to say. Her voice trailed off.

"Yes, it is," Meg sighed. "You've probably been going back over all those times he told you he loved you and couldn't live without you."

"Right," Hannah agreed, hoping she'd drop it. "That's exactly right."

Meg snorted. "And you believed him?"

*Yes, I did, because, stupid me, I always believed everything Kurt told me—I always knew without a single doubt in my mind that Kurt would never lie to me—that everything Kurt promises, he does, no matter what—*

"He's such a jerk." Meg frowned. "I've always been kind of scared of him." She gazed out the kitchen window and added, "It's probably a good thing the weather's so bad. Knowing him, he might come out here and try to break in the house or something."

Hannah tried to suppress a shiver, but Meg threw her a worried look.

"He wouldn't, would he, Han?"

"Of course not." Somehow Hannah managed to sound convincing. "Honestly, Meg, sometimes you get the dumbest ideas. Get those hot dogs ready—I'm going to check on Jonathon."

Gratefully Hannah escaped. She stopped outside the living room and collected herself for a moment, not sure what she might find inside.

Jonathon was lying on the couch. His eyes were closed; he was pale and very still. Lance had propped his leg on some pillows and covered him with a blanket.

Thinking he was asleep, Hannah started to back away when Jonathon suddenly opened his eyes. He stared at her, then with a wan smile, motioned her in. Hannah noticed his jeans hanging over the back of a chair . . . his sweater folded on top. The fire crackled softly, throwing shadows over his tousled hair and the weary lines of his face.

Jonathon patted the edge of the couch. "I'd ask you to sit, but I'm not quite presentable," he murmured.

Hannah smiled and sat anyway. "Don't be silly. I grew up with a brother, remember? I don't shock easily."

"Still . . ." Jonathon teased, "I hardly know you."

"I'll loan you my dad's robe," Hannah promised. "Or my nightshirt, if you'd rather. How do you feel?"

"Terrific. Let's race."

"How about eating instead?"

"How about not."

"Meg wants to roast hot dogs in the fireplace. Is that okay?"

Jonathon looked amused. "Why are you asking me? It's your house."

"Well, right now it's your hospital room," Hannah corrected him. Her eyes fell to the blanket, to his leg propped up on the pillows. "Did it hurt?" she asked softly.

"Over before I even knew."

"Are you telling the truth?"

Jonathon sighed. "No. It hurt like hell."

"I didn't hear you make any noise at all."

"I gagged him," Lance said, coming into the room. As Hannah started, he gave an innocent shrug. "Sorry. Just a little torture humor."

"He didn't gag me," Jonathon assured her. "And the reason you didn't hear me make any noise was 'cause I had that pillow over my face the whole time."

Suddenly Hannah wanted to laugh. She looked down at him and felt a hundred conflicting emotions go through her.

"You're so brave," she said, deadpan.

"It's a hero thing," Jonathon agreed, then added almost sheepishly, "The truth is, I moaned a lot."

Lance walked over to the fireplace. He stabbed at the logs with the poker, coaxing the flames higher.

"He needs to get his strength back," Lance said, keeping his back to them. "He's weak, and his resistance is low. Prime candidate for infection."

"Such a positive prognosis," Jonathon sighed. "I feel better already." As Lance turned to leave, Jonathon caught hold of his arm. "Thanks," he mumbled.

Lance looked down at him, a long silent stare.

"We're even," he said quietly, and walked out of the room.

For a moment no one spoke. Then Hannah patted Jonathon lightly on his shoulder.

"Lance is right about keeping up your strength," she insisted. "At least try and get something down." The look he gave her was so pathetic that she had to laugh. "Okay, okay, no hot dogs. But I'm sure we have some steaks in the freezer. Red meat would be good for you, wouldn't it?"

"If you say so."

"Try and get some rest. I'll be back in a while."

Jonathon nodded. His eyelids were heavy, and Hannah slipped out of the room, hoping he'd sleep while she was gone. She hesitated on the basement stairs, shining her flashlight into the corners, annoyed with herself for feeling afraid. Forcing herself to go down, she quickly found the steaks and brought them up to the kitchen. Then she pulled on her coat and went outside.

*Kurt.*

No matter how she tried, she couldn't get him out of her mind—his awful threats—the scene in the garage and up in Meg's bedroom. She trudged through the falling snow, threading her way between the thick shrubbery that hugged the back of the house. Drifts had piled up—some as high as the first-floor windows. *Maybe he did climb up to Meg's room . . . but how?*

She stopped beneath her sister's window and studied the lay of the roof. Lance was right—there were plenty of places to hold on, plenty of ways to go up. All anyone had to do was make it to the overhang of the porch, and from there it would be an easy matter to use tree branches and jutting gables. And even if the intruder made noise, no one would pay attention,

Hannah thought grimly—not with all the other noises the old house made.

*If I could just get up there over the porch . . .*

Quickly Hannah scanned her surroundings, looking for something to boost her up. The picnic table had been pushed back against the house and covered up for the winter, but Hannah pulled it out again and climbed on top. By stretching as far as she could, she was just able to reach the overhang. She gave a little hop and caught hold, but couldn't quite swing herself up. Frustrated, she dropped down again and tried to think what to do.

She spotted a folded lawn chair in one corner of the porch. She opened it and set it on top of the picnic table, then she climbed up and swung herself onto the roof.

It was a lot more slippery than it looked.

Lying there slantwise, Hannah chided herself for having such a stupid idea. She held her breath and inched sideways until she could reach a tree limb. She pulled herself to the trunk, hugged it tightly, and began to climb.

It was awkward going up—not to mention cold and slippery—but she forced herself on till she reached the ledge under Meg's window. She leaned in close to the screen, trying to peer through thick layers of frost into the room beyond.

Everything was dark. It was almost impossible to distinguish anything in the shadows. Hannah lowered her eyes and felt a stab of fear shoot through her.

The corner of the screen was away from the window.

As though someone had pried it loose, trying to get inside.

*Or has it always been this way?*

As Hannah bent closer, she could see tiny red droplets frozen to the edge of the windowsill, mixed in with the clinging snow.

*Blood?*

Recoiling in alarm, Hannah forgot how narrow the ledge was. For one second she flailed wildly, scrabbling at the window, but then she felt herself sliding down, without even a chance to scream.

As she hurtled toward the ground below, she grabbed for the tree and missed—grabbed desperately for a thin strip of gutter—

Her feet went off into nothingness.

There was one split second of unreality, and as she dangled there from the edge of the roof, her fingers began to slip away.

**14**

"Hannah!"

Someone was calling her. She fought back the rear and tightened her hold on the gutter.

"What?" she called back weakly. Her fingers were throbbing.

"Hannah!" the voice shouted again, only more insistent this time.

Hannah looked down through the swirling whiteness.

She could see Lance making his way along the back of the house, and he sounded mad.

"I'm right here!" she shouted.

He stopped right below her. He put his hands on his hips and tilted his head back and just stared up at her where she dangled from the roof.

"Jesus Christ! What are you doing up—"

A loud cracking sound cut him off. Hannah felt

something give beneath her fingers, and she braced herself to fall.

"Hang on!" Lance called.

"I'm trying to—I don't think I can!"

"Then let go! I'll catch you."

"No!" She could feel herself going into a panic. She was trying so hard to hang on, but somehow her left hand wasn't cooperating anymore.

"Hannah—"

"No! I'm scared!"

She didn't know what she expected, exactly—for him to comfort her, perhaps, or reassure her, for him to swing right up there beside her and carry her down to safety. But certainly not the reaction she got.

"Okay." Lance shrugged. "Fall, then."

To her astonishment, he turned and headed back. Hannah gritted her teeth and felt her muscles lock in one last, futile attempt to hold on.

"No—come back!" she pleaded. "I could break something!"

"You're not going to break anything," he said calmly. "Drop down."

She didn't have a choice. She could see him there below her—windblown hair—graceful stance—poised and ready. . . .

Hannah closed her eyes and took a deep breath.

"Trust me," Lance said.

Her eyes flew open. In desperation she clutched at the roof, but felt herself falling helplessly down.

He cushioned her with his body. They rolled together in the snow, and she lay there, stunned, looking up at him, his body sprawled lengthwise on top of hers, his face just inches from her own. His hair blew softly against her cheeks, as soft as his breath on her skin, and as Hannah gazed into his narrowed eyes, she had the sudden, unsettling impression that he was reading her most intimate thoughts.

"Are you crazy?" Hannah raged at him. "You could have killed me!"

"Killed you?" Lance retorted smoothly. "You're the one who was crazy enough to climb up there on the roof."

"I had to see—" Hannah stammered, "I was trying to see—"

"Yes?"

And he was laughing at her—she *knew* it—even though his voice was deep and solemn, even though he gazed down at her with those black, black eyes and no expression at all on his face. She squirmed beneath him, then caught her breath and stopped. She could feel her cheeks going warm—as warm as every spot where she and Lance were touching.

"Yes?" he prompted her. "You were trying to see something?"

"The—the—window," she tried again, hating herself for being flustered, hating him even more for knowing it. "Get off me," she said sharply.

Lance seemed to consider this a moment, looking down at her with a relentless stare. Hannah felt her breath quickening—her heart racing. Once more she tried to move, once more she stopped, all too aware of his body on hers. Then she saw one corner of his mouth curl in a sardonic smile.

"You know . . ." Lance murmured, "if I wasn't so sure what an in-control person you are . . . I'd swear you were blushing."

"Let me go!" Hannah screamed, and tried to swing at him.

Without warning, he pinned her hands to the ground. He was so incredibly strong that Hannah felt a surge of panic go through her—she twisted from side to side, but she might as well have been a butterfly in a net. Gasping, she felt Lance crush her down into the snow, and his eyes flashed above her with a strange, dark light.

"Oh, I forgot," he said quietly. "You don't like being this close to escaped killers, do you?"

Hannah gasped in terror. She could see the tense lines of his cheeks, the endless dark of his eyes. As she gazed up helplessly, she could feel her lips moving, trying to get out the words.

"I don't know what you mean," she whispered. "I—I don't know what you're talking about—"

"Oh . . . I think you do."

"It's—it's just that I was on the roof—and I was so—so scared—"

"You don't know what scared is."

Without warning, he rolled off.

"Oh. And by the way . . . I tried to start your car, but nothing worked. Guess you really *are* stranded now."

Hannah lay there, listening to his boots crunch through the snow, back along the house and to the porch. The door slammed, and the world was cold and silent.

*Jonathon! Jonathon must have told him what I said!*

She felt giddy from the aftershock of fear. She lay there for several minutes, totally oblivious to the cold. At last she stood up and shakily began brushing snow from her clothes.

*Jonathon must have told Lance everything—all my suspicions about him—and the two of them must have laughed and laughed—what a joke on Hannah—*

She was furious with herself—furious for having trusted Jonathon—furious for being vulnerable to Lance. Lance—she *hated* him! She *despised* him!

*"You're fascinated with him because you're afraid of him."*

Her earlier words to Meg hit Hannah like a slap. Angrily she turned and kicked through the bushes at the side of the house. And then, as her foot made contact with something, she looked down and stared.

She could see wires hanging there, attached to the house. Useless wires dangling down in the snow.

Slowly Hannah reached over and picked up the ends.

And it came to her then, in a slow, chilling awareness, the *real* reason why all the phone lines were dead. . . .

Someone had cut them.

# 15

Dazed, Hannah started back for the house.

*Then that means whoever cut them did it last night—before the boys even got here. So that means someone really is watching the house—*

*Kurt? The escaped killer?*

Hannah shook her head. She stopped and gazed off across the yard . . . to the woodpile . . . to the tree stump where the axe was still missing. . . .

*Or did the phone lines really go out because of the storm? And then, after Jonathon and Lance got here, Lance cut the wires so that even if the phones came back on again, there'd be no way we could ever call for help. . . .*

She climbed up onto the porch. She could see Meg through the kitchen window chattering happily to Lance, who was slouched in a chair and drinking a fresh cup of coffee.

*I can't leave her in there alone. I have to stay with her every minute. . . .*

Without warning, Lance shifted in his chair. He turned and looked straight out the window, straight at her, and unconsciously Hannah took a step back into the corner. *It's like he knows I'm out here—like he knew I'd be standing right there at that precise second in that precise spot, and he's taking his time and he's enjoying this. . . .*

She forced herself to go to the door. Then suddenly she felt her feet turning her around and taking her toward the driveway.

*I'll go look for Bruce. I'll look out in front. I'll just stay out for a second—*

She felt a surge of panic go through her. Fear—confusion—responsibility—everything tangled inside her till she felt like she might explode. She had to think. She had to think what to do.

*Bruce. First I'll try and find Bruce.*

Cupping her hands around her mouth, she yelled the dog's name. The call echoed back to her through the falling snow, but there was no answering bark. *I wonder where that stupid dog's wandered off to?*

"Nothing's happened to him," she muttered fiercely. "He's just lost, that's all. He'll turn up. Please, God, he has to turn up."

She didn't want to admit to Meg—or herself—just how worried she was getting about him. Even with his heavy coat, it was way too cold for him to be out this long, and with his fading senses, he could have wandered off in any direction and gotten hopelessly disoriented. *If he stays out tonight, will he freeze to death?*

Hannah felt tears spring to her eyes. *Stupid dog . . . as if I didn't have enough to worry about!*

She marched determinedly down the drive, down the hill that sloped from the front of the house. Could something else have caused those phone lines to be cut? she wondered desperately. Maybe some animal chewed on them. Maybe the wind blew them loose. . . .

*You are* really *grabbing at straws, aren't you?*

"Kurt," Hannah told herself firmly. "It had to have been Kurt."

What had he been planning to do to them once the phones were out? she worried now. And if that was really the case, why hadn't he carried out his plan?

*Another thing I can't tell Meg.*

Hannah stopped, her eyes moving slowly across the trees, the road, the surrounding hills. Everything was frozen and still. The storm had come, and life had stopped.

Hannah burrowed deeper into her coat and kept on. Maybe Bruce had gone wandering off down the road. He was used to meeting the school bus every afternoon—maybe he'd gotten confused and gone looking for Meg.

Hannah felt sick and scared and alone.

"Bruce!" she shouted. "Bruce, where are you?"

If anything happened to that dumb dog, Meg would be inconsolable. *So you're out here looking for him while she's back at the house with that crazy Lance and that traitor Jonathon—*

"Bruce!" she screamed. "Come on, boy—dinnertime!"

Fear pulled her in a thousand different directions.

*What am I doing? Bruce couldn't hear an explosion if it happened right under him.*

She walked as far as the end of the drive. From there the road sloped up to the left, and down again to the right, followed by a series of wide turns weaving off between thick clumps of trees.

"Bruce!"

Shivering from more than the cold, Hannah stepped out into the road, turning first one way, then the other. Opting for the downhill trek, she promised herself she would only search for ten more minutes, then get right back to the house.

She didn't really expect to see anything at all.

So when she spotted the car headed up the slope toward their house, at first she thought she must be dreaming. Then, with a jolt of relief, she started running to meet it.

"Hey! Hey! Over here! We need help!"

Laughing, she scrambled closer. *God, all that worry for nothing—Lance and Jonathon were just two innocent guys, and Kurt tried to scare me, but then he felt bad about it and went on his trip, and escaped mental patients only happen in movies, and this driver probably picked up Bruce in his car and is trying to find out where he lives, and Mom and Dad'll probably be home tomorrow because the snow will stop—*

Hannah stopped in confusion.

She'd been so sure the car was coming to the house . . . but now, as she stared at it, she realized it wasn't coming at all.

It wasn't even moving.

In fact, now that she was closer, she could see that it was tilted at a weird angle and stuck in the snow-covered ditch at the side of the road.

Her heart fell to her toes.

She just stood there and stared.

And then . . . slowly . . . she realized she'd seen that car before.

*Kurt! That's Kurt's car!*

Hannah started to run. Slipping and sliding, she finally reached the car, then she ran up to the driver's side, not knowing what she might find.

The door was partway open.

Snow had blown in, coating the seat and dash with ice.

But the car was empty.

# 16

"Meg!"

Hannah slammed the kitchen door, stamping snow off her boots. After being out for so long, the house felt warm despite its lack of heat, and she stood for a moment, almost giddy, as the blood started flowing again through her veins.

"Meg! Where are you?"

"We're in here!" her sister called back.

Hannah went to the living room, peeling off her gloves and coat. Jonathon was still on the couch, his eyes closed. Meg and Lance sat together on the floor, roasting marshmallows in the fireplace.

"What is it?" Meg asked. She caught the disapproving look Hannah gave her, and immediately was on the defensive. "What do you want?"

"Kurt's car," Hannah said breathlessly.

"What about it?"

"I found Kurt's car!"

Meg looked puzzled. She pulled her stick back from the flames. "Where?"

"Just down the road. It looks like he was probably coming here. But he's not in his car—and it's not like him to go off and leave it like that. Especially with the door open."

"Unless he left in a hurry," Jonathon murmured, and Hannah's voice went tight.

"What's that supposed to mean?"

Lance shrugged. "He might have been in trouble."

"The car was off the road . . . sideways in the ditch."

"Do you think he slid?" Meg asked. "He might have gotten out to see how bad he was stuck."

"Then where is he?" Hannah demanded. "If he got out, he would have come here. So what happened to him?"

Meg looked at her. Then she looked at Lance, who calmly redirected his gaze to the fire.

"Isn't anyone worried but me?" Hannah burst out.

"Well . . ." Meg said truthfully, her eyes wide and solemn, "you're the only one who likes him, Hannah."

"I can't believe this!" Hannah fumed. "He might be lying out there hurt or—or—"

"Correct me if I'm wrong," Lance said dryly. "But is this the same psychopath who threatened to kill you?"

"What!" Meg squeaked. "He did *what?*"

"I asked you not to say anything!" Furiously Hannah turned on Lance. "I asked you not to, and you deliberately—" She broke off, wheeling to Jonathon. "And you! When we talked, I didn't expect you to repeat everything I said!"

"What?" Jonathon turned his head to look at her. "What are you talking about?"

"You know what I'm talking about!" Hannah cried. "And I hope you two had fun laughing at me!"

"Oh, you discussed me with Jonathon, too?" Lance said smoothly, raising an eyebrow. "Well, I'm sure he'll be able to protect you from me in the shape he's in."

For a split second Hannah looked completely bewildered. Then she turned slowly to Meg.

"You," she said icily, but Meg was trying to make herself invisible, pulling herself into a tight, little ball, staring at Hannah with huge, round eyes.

"All I said," she insisted, "was I didn't think he looked much like an escaped—"

"Shut up, Meg. I think you've said plenty."

"But, Hannah, I didn't mean—"

"Wait." Jonathon's voice sounded weakly from the couch, and the other three turned, as if they'd forgotten he was there. He struggled up into a half-sitting position and shook his head at Hannah. "I think Lance is absolutely right. After what your boyfriend left in the garage last night, how do you know he didn't just abandon his car to scare you?"

Meg looked totally baffled. "What are you talking about?"

"He slashed up her sweater," Lance said, while Hannah glared at him. "Along with a disemboweled rat."

Meg's face drained white. "Why didn't you tell me!" she wailed. "Oh, Hannah—does that mean he's done something to Bruce!"

Meg promptly burst into tears. Jonathon groaned.

Hannah swore under her breath, and Lance, after a split second of indecision, began to stab the fire angrily with the poker.

"Hannah!" Meg sobbed. "Oh, Hannah, if anything happens to Bruce—"

"Are you satisfied?" Hannah fairly spat at Lance.

"Hey, come on." Jonathon tried to sound cheerful. "Nothing's going to happen to Bruce. He'll come home."

"Promise?" Meg pleaded.

"What are we going to do about Kurt?" Hannah broke in quickly.

Jonathon laid one arm wearily across his forehead. "What *can* we do?"

"Search the woods, maybe. Or—or—maybe he passed up the house somehow walking in the dark, and he's farther down the road or something—"

"The guy threatened to kill you," Jonathon said softly, "and you're worried if he's hurt."

"He wouldn't have hurt me!" Hannah insisted.

"Right, I forgot. Just your sweater."

"You don't know." Lance finally spoke again, slowly, from the shadows across the room. "People like that . . . you never know what could set them off."

"He's crazy," Meg said softly. "I've never liked him."

Hannah shook her head. "He was just upset. I *know* him—he'll get over it."

"People like that . . ." Lance murmured, "you never know what they'll get over. What they'll remember." He glanced toward the window, his voice lowering even more. "They don't *need* a reason to do things. Or a conscience."

141

"Some of them do," Jonathon said. He lay there staring at the ceiling, his voice soft and distant . . . as though the effort of talking was just too great. "Some of them know the difference between right and wrong."

"But the fine line is," Lance added, "they think they're always right."

For a moment Jonathon was silent. Then he said softly, "Yeah. Something like that."

Hannah stared at Meg's bowed head. She set her jaw determinedly.

"Well, I'm going to look for him," she declared. "Whether any of you come or not."

"I don't think you should be walking anywhere out there by yourself," Jonathon said. "Especially not now. What if he's *not* hurt? What if he really *is* hiding somewhere watching the house, like we thought before? Just waiting for a chance to get you alone?"

"I've been out alone already," she insisted, "and nothing happened."

"How do you know?" Lance asked slowly, and she turned to face him.

"How do I know what?"

"That you were really alone?"

"I can't stand this!" Meg's voice rose, and she clamped her hands over her ears. "You're all *scaring* me! I feel like crazy people are going to start crashing through the windows any second!"

For a moment there was silence.

Then Jonathon softly began to laugh.

Lance looked almost startled, and then a slow smile played over one corner of his mouth.

And then, helplessly, Hannah felt her own mouth move in a smile.

"Don't worry, Meg." Jonathon winked at her. "We won't let anyone get you."

"Oh, I can take care of myself," Meg retorted tearfully. She hurried out of the room, and a second later they heard the bathroom door slam upstairs.

Hannah stood there a minute, and then she sighed. "I hope you're both satisfied. She's going to get hysterical."

"She's worried about her dog," Lance said quietly.

"I know she is."

"I'm going to look for him."

Hannah turned to him in surprise. "You mean you're going out to look for that stupid dog and not Kurt?"

He didn't answer. He disappeared down the hall, and Hannah heard the back door.

"But—but you don't understand!" She turned to Jonathon. "He'd never leave his car like that—it just doesn't make sense—"

"Crazy people don't make sense," Jonathon murmured. He turned his head and gazed at her for a long, silent moment, then at last put his head back on the pillow and closed his eyes. "I just told you," he whispered.

Hannah felt cold. The fire flickered softly, casting shadows over the wall and Jonathon's face. He looked almost as though he were wearing a mask, delicately carved from white bone. Shivering, she turned her back on him and went upstairs.

She found Meg in the bathroom, staring out the window at the snow.

"It's coming down harder now," she choked, tears

streaming down her face, "and poor Bruce won't be able to find his way home. . . ."

"Yes, he will," Hannah insisted, sitting down on the edge of the tub. "He *will*. He's done it before."

"He's probably wondering why we haven't come looking for him—"

"Stop it, Meg. Lance is going out to search."

"Really?" Meg sniffled.

"Really."

For a moment Meg was silent. Then slowly she raised her eyes and fixed them on Hannah's face.

"How come you never told me about Kurt?"

"I didn't want to scare you."

"Did he really say he was going to kill you?"

"Oh, you know Kurt—he was just talking. In a day or two, he'll have a new girlfriend, and he won't even remember who I am."

Meg stared at her and said nothing. Hannah gave her a quick hug and went back down to the living room. The heaters were working, but the room was getting colder . . . just as the whole house was getting colder. She paused beside the couch and gazed down at Jonathon's face. He stirred slightly, then as if sensing her presence, slowly opened his eyes.

"How do you feel?" Hannah asked him. "Really?"

He frowned and shook his head. Then he slowly reached out and took hold of her hand.

"Lance remembered," he said softly, and Hannah leaned closer to hear.

"Remembered what?" she asked him.

"The picture by your bed. I thought you should know."

"Jonathon, you're not making any sense at all—"

"The guy in the picture," he insisted. "Your boy-friend."

"What about him?"

"When Lance was hitchhiking last night." A frown settled over Jonathon's face. "Kurt was the one who gave him a ride."

# 17

"The car on the bridge? The one who caused your wreck?" Hannah asked, shocked. "Are you sure?"

Jonathon nodded. "Lance said the driver was all bundled up . . . but from what he could see of his face—"

"Then he can't be positive," Hannah said almost defiantly. "He can't really be sure."

Jonathon looked at her, baffled. "Why are you defending Kurt?" he murmured. "After all he's done?"

"I—" Hannah stopped. She didn't know why. Maybe it was all those months of asking herself why she put up with Kurt and trying to figure out why she needed him so much. She looked down at Jonathon, and her face softened . . . went sad. "I don't know," she said at last.

Jonathon smiled. He took her hand and gave it a gentle squeeze.

"It's okay," he said.

Their eyes met and held. Hannah felt a lump rise into her throat, and she quickly began smoothing the covers over him.

"Get some rest," she said. "I'm going to get more blankets."

He nodded at her, his fingers sliding from her arm. In spite of the cold, he felt unusually warm, and Hannah wondered anxiously if he was running a fever. She turned away, her mind racing. *Kurt stopped to give Lance a ride ... Kurt caused Jonathon's accident ... Kurt took off and left them both to freeze to death ...*

*Or is Lance making it all up?*

Troubled, Hannah wandered into the kitchen. Maybe Kurt had never given Lance a ride at all. And if he had, maybe it was Lance who'd caused the car to skid in the first place. . . .

*Or maybe it's Jonathon. Maybe Jonathon's lying ... about everything—*

Angrily Hannah squeezed her eyes shut and gripped the edge of the countertop.

"Hannah?"

Hannah swung around and saw Meg standing behind her. For a second the two sisters looked at each other, then Meg gave Hannah a hug.

"Maybe . . ." Meg suggested helpfully, "maybe . . . Kurt got a ride with someone else. Maybe some of his dumb friends followed him out here, and they put that stuff in the garage, and then when Kurt's car got stuck, he went with the others."

Hannah didn't answer. She turned to the window and stared out through the whirling snow.

"I know what you're thinking," Meg sighed, sitting

down at the table, propping her chin in her hands. "You're thinking maybe he died, and he's lying out there buried somewhere—"

Again an image of the woodpile formed in her mind—again Hannah forced it away.

"Well, thanks, Meg, that's very consoling." Hannah pulled on her coat and gloves and went out the back door. "And so like you!"

"Wait!" Meg yelled. "Hannah, don't go out there and start looking around! I'm sorry I said that!"

Hannah took off across the yard. She heard Meg run out on the porch and yell after her, but she deliberately ignored her.

*Oh, God . . . what am I going to do . . . ?*

Images flashed through her mind—Kurt wounded, Kurt frozen to death . . . lying lifeless beneath layers and layers of snow. Kurt trying to get to her house, trying to get help—

"Where are you going?"

She stifled a scream as Lance grabbed her elbow and spun her around. She hit out at him, but he caught her effortlessly by the wrist.

"Let go of me! I've got to find my boyfriend!"

"Your boyfriend? The maniac?"

"You don't know anything about him!"

"I don't want to know anything about him."

"Look, just because he did something stupid doesn't mean we shouldn't help him!"

Lance hesitated. His eyes swept the yard—the house—the woods at their back.

"I've got to find him!" Hannah insisted.

"You're not going to find anybody out here," Lance told her. "It's getting dark, and the wind's worse than ever. If you go running off, we'll be out here trying to find *you!*"

"You don't understand—he might have been coming to the house trying to get help—"

"Help." He nodded, eyes narrowing. "Right. A dead rat in the car and a sweater you'll never be able to wear again. He needs help, all right, but not from you."

"You don't have any business saying—"

"And you don't have any business being out here in this weather." Lance's grip tightened on her arm, and Hannah winced.

"And what about you?" she threw back at him. "What are you doing every time you come out here? How come you just disappear sometimes and then show up again, and nobody seems to know where you've been?"

She could swear that something flashed deep in his eyes—something fierce and dangerous and barely, barely controlled. He stepped closer to her, and instinctively she tried to move away.

"I didn't realize I needed your permission to come and go," he said between clenched teeth. "But if you're so worried about it"—his hand squeezed steadily on her arm, and she caught her breath in alarm—"why don't you just follow me sometime?"

Hannah jerked free. She rubbed her arm and stumbled back out of his reach.

"That boyfriend of yours." Lance drew a deep breath. "He could be miles away by now. Gloating over how much you're obsessed with him."

"I'm not obsessed with—"

"You're obsessed. Forget it—you don't need him."

"You don't know what I need. And you don't know anything about obsessions."

"Don't I?" A laugh sounded deep in his throat . . . a laugh that chilled Hannah to the bone. He stared at her for so long that she moved back once again, trying to escape the relentless scrutiny of his eyes. "Oh, I know about obsessions, all right," he murmured. "They take over your life. They make you become what they are. They—"

He stopped abruptly. His eyes flicked from Hannah's face to the house, then back again in one swift glance. For a split second she had the eerie feeling he'd surveyed the whole backyard, as well, and the darkening sky and the hidden depths of the woods.

"What is it?" she asked.

Without a word, Lance turned and walked away.

"If you're trying to scare me, it won't work!" Hannah declared hotly.

She stood and watched him go. She thought about Kurt and his abandoned car, and she racked her brain in desperation, wondering what she was going to do. He'd sounded drunk when he'd threatened her yesterday—that would certainly explain all his bizarre behavior—and if he hadn't been coherent when he'd left the garage last night, then there was no telling where he might have wandered off . . . what might have happened to him.

*To him and Bruce,* Hannah thought wryly—except Bruce seemed to be getting a whole lot more sympathy from everyone. She tilted her head and looked up into the sky, shielding her eyes from the snow. Lance was right—the wind was picking up something fierce. She wondered if it would ever stop snowing again.

She saw Lance head off into the woods. She heard

his deep voice yelling Bruce's name. Reluctantly she went back down the drive and followed the road until she got to Kurt's car. Drifts lay thick around it, and she eyed the scene as one might view something in a dream. Her breath came in short gasps; she was freezing cold. She didn't know how much longer she could stay out.

*Someone could be hidden under all that snow. . . . It's deep enough. . . .*

She bent down and ran her hands over the smooth, white surface. She had a wild thought that somehow she might feel a heartbeat or hear a faint voice calling for help. She didn't even realize she'd started to dig until suddenly she touched something and cried out in fear.

For a moment Hannah stood there transfixed.

Slowly . . . carefully . . . she flexed her fingers and worked her hand deeper, pushing the drift apart.

And she *had* felt something—she was sure of it now—something long and solid, lying there beneath quiet layers of snow—just lying there and not moving—

It came free so quickly, it threw her off balance.

And as Hannah fell to the ground, her only thought was that the thing she'd discovered was still clutched tightly in her hand. . . .

# 18

Hannah stared down at it, her whole body going weak

*A tree branch?*

A tree branch as big around as a man's arm, stuck there in the snow beside Kurt's car.

Hannah felt sick with relief.

Backing away, she stared at the shapeless mounds of snow piled around her, a feeling of helplessness gnawing the pit of her stomach. *Could someone really be buried under there? Would I be able to tell?*

In growing despair she turned and made her way back along the road, her eyes scanning the wooded landscape as she went. *He could be anywhere out there—anywhere.*

"Kurt!" she screamed. "Where are you!"

She didn't dare go into the woods; she knew it'd be nearly impossible finding her way in this weather. Snow filled the air like a thick white fog, and the wind shifted the landscape before her very eyes.

*Oh, please let him be okay. Please let him be skiing right this very minute . . . or curled up in front of a roaring fire with his new girlfriend. . . .*

Even a new girlfriend was easier for Hannah to take than the thought of Kurt stalking her—or the possibility that some tragedy had occurred. *I just wanted to break up with him . . . I didn't want anything bad to happen. . . .*

Hannah looked toward the house. Someone was standing in the front window waving at her to come inside. Sighing, she trudged home and sat down on the kitchen floor to wrestle off her boots.

Her eyes slowly swept the kitchen counter. She saw the steaks she'd left out, and she mentally began to plan dinner. Funny . . . there were only three steaks thawing, and she could have sworn she'd brought up four earlier from the freezer. *Oh, well, I'll just fix myself some soup.* Her first thought was to blame Bruce, but then she remembered that Bruce wasn't here. . . .

She covered her face with her hands and ordered herself not to cry. She didn't think she'd ever felt *more* like crying in her life, yet at the same time her heart felt bruised and empty. She lifted her head and realized with a start that someone was standing there looking down at her.

"You need to eat something," Lance said.

"Yes. I'll start dinner in a little while."

"I didn't mean for you to *fix* dinner. I just want you to *eat* it."

Hannah got up. She unbuttoned her coat and let the sleeves fall slowly down her arms. Lance sighed and folded his arms across his chest.

"There's nothing you can do," Lance said. There

was no anger this time . . . no annoyance. Hannah glanced at him suspiciously, and he added, "Come and get warm."

She gave a vague nod. She went to the living room and found Meg telling Jonathon all about Bruce while he listened from the couch with a tolerant smile. As Hannah settled herself on the hearth, Meg came and sat beside her.

"Don't you think as long as we're all stuck here together, we should get to know each other?" Meg asked. When Hannah shook her head, Meg went ahead anyway. "Lance, you go first."

Lance barely flicked a glance at her. After several seconds, Meg tried again.

"You know . . . like where you're from?"

"I don't like to talk about myself," Lance said.

Meg stared at him. "Well . . . okay, I'll think of something else. What do you do when you're camping?"

Lance turned to look at her. He held her eyes in a long, silent stare. At last Meg swallowed and smiled at Jonathon.

"Okay. How about you?"

"I don't think this is a very good game," Hannah interrupted. "Why don't you go read or something?"

"I can read anytime," Meg said. "I'd rather sit here and talk."

Hannah understood. Anything was better than sitting and worrying about Bruce. *Or Kurt . . .*

She turned to Jonathon. "How are you feeling?"

"Oh, you know. Fine." He looked at her a minute, then shook his head. "Sorry," he mumbled. "I wish I could help."

"Well, I better go start dinner."

She unwrapped the steaks and stood looking down at them, her stomach going queasy at the sight of raw meat. She felt like she was going to explode. She leaned on the kitchen counter and stared miserably out at the swirling void of a world. *We'll never get out of here. We'll never get out, and nobody will ever find us. I'm in charge—what a joke!*

*A joke . . .*

Slowly she straightened, lips tightening. *Kurt's car by the side of the road . . . just like the sweater and the rat in the car . . .* Could it be he was just trying to play another joke on her? She'd always known his sense of humor was sick and twisted . . . but would he really have gone this far? With a sinking heart she realized he would, that true to form, Kurt would stop at nothing to get back at someone who'd let him down. . . .

She lowered her head and groaned. What a laugh he must be having right now. And she'd stood out there for who knows how long, till her body froze and her muscles ached, digging through the drifts like a ridiculous fool. . . .

*I am ridiculous. I've been ridiculous the whole time. Kurt . . . escaped killers . . . deranged strangers sharing my house . . .*

*Come on, Hannah, pull yourself together.*

She forced herself through menial tasks—wrapping potatoes in foil, putting them in the oven, seasoning the steaks. She didn't want to go back in there with the others right now . . . she couldn't stand to talk or even think. She felt numb and exhausted from too much worry and fear.

She dreaded nightfall, but it came all too quickly. They lit candles and lanterns, while Lance kept vigil with the heaters. They closed the curtains for added insulation. They huddled around the fireplace trying to make small talk.

"We should all sleep in here tonight," Lance said. "Shut off the other rooms to keep this one warmer."

Hannah didn't want to sleep in the same room with everyone else, but she knew Lance was right. With outside temperatures plummeting, they had to conserve heat where they could. Jonathon offered to sleep on the floor, but she and Meg overruled him. Once more Hannah made a trip to the garage, this time with Lance to bring back sleeping bags. Meg gathered up all the pillows and blankets from the upstairs beds. Lance stretched out on one side of the fireplace, Meg curled up in the recliner, and Hannah spread her blankets on the floor near Meg's chair.

Minutes dragged like hours. Muffled sobs came from Meg's chair, and Hannah knew she was still thinking about Bruce. It was all Hannah could do not to cry herself—Bruce had never been gone this long before, and with temperatures this bitter, she feared the worst come morning. She put her pillow over her head, but she could still hear Jonathon's ragged breathing as he shifted restlessly in his sleep. She gazed up at the ceiling and was suddenly aware of movement near the fire. Turning on her side, she watched Lance stir the coals and fan the flames, trying to coax more heat out into the room.

He crawled over to Jonathon's side. Hannah saw the shadowy outline of his hand as he touched it to Jonathon's forehead. Jonathon moaned softly. Lance murmured something she couldn't hear . . . hesitated . . . then moved back to sit at the opposite end of the fireplace.

"Is he all right?" Hannah whispered.

For a moment there was silence. Then finally she saw Lance nod.

Quiet filled the room again . . . shadows flickered softly over the walls.

"Can't you sleep?" Hannah asked at last.

She saw his head move again.

"Me neither," she sighed.

Stretching, she crawled from her sleeping bag and nearer the fire. Lance didn't acknowledge her. He leaned back and gazed into the darkness. Hannah stared at him, watching black shadows flow over his hair . . . watching the flames of the fire reflect in the depths of his eyes.

She followed the direction of his gaze and realized with a start that he was looking at Meg.

"She's exhausted," Hannah said quickly, hoping to distract him.

Lance nodded. Keeping his eyes on Meg, he leaned his head back against the wall.

"Innocents," he said softly, as Hannah strained to hear him.

"What did you say?"

"Innocents. They're always the ones caught."

Silence settled between them. Hannah shivered softly.

"You mean . . . the ones who suffer?" she whispered, and saw his head move slowly in a nod.

"Yes. Like the animals."

"I . . . I don't know what to say about—" Hannah began, but it was as if Lance didn't hear.

"Wouldn't it be great," he murmured, "if the guilty ones could pay. If the bad ones could all be punished."

A slow chill crept through her. She wanted to

answer him, to make him explain, but she couldn't seem to find her voice. Lance sat like a statue. Dim light and shadow played over the angles of his face, yet Hannah could tell he was still staring through the darkness at Meg as she slept.

He whispered something . . . one word.

To Hannah it sounded almost like "sweet," but she couldn't be sure.

Still trembling, she pulled her blanket close around her shoulders and glanced uneasily around the room. It didn't seem safe to her anymore . . . or familiar. Like somebody else's house she'd never seen or been in . . . a place of hidden secrets and dangers.

"He needs a doctor," Lance said softly, and she jumped at the sound of his voice.

"Who?" Hannah asked. "Jonathon?"

"I'm afraid he's getting worse."

"Are you sure? How do you know that?"

Lance didn't answer. Hannah tried again.

"You . . . you said you've worked at a hospital. But you never said what kind."

At last he moved his eyes.

He shifted them to Hannah's face and fixed them there, so that her heart began to pound and the chill in her veins was like a slow, cold death. . . .

"The worst kind," he murmured. "Where no one ever gets well."

"You mean"—Hannah swallowed hard, forcing herself to ask, forcing herself to press him, but not sure she really wanted to know—"people are in there just to . . . to die?"

He held her with an unblinking stare. His voice was hollow and strangely resigned.

158

"You can't die if you're already dead."

He didn't turn away. He didn't move at all.

It was Hannah who finally crept back to bed.

She climbed into her sleeping bag and watched his silhouette against the writhing flames of the fire.

She wasn't sure he even knew she'd left him.

# 19

"Hannah . . ."

Meg's voice cut through layers and layers of sleep. With a cry, Hannah bolted upright and looked around in a panic. The room was throbbing with noiseless shadows . . . each corner deceptively alive. For one second she couldn't remember where she was, or why she was here, but then as her eyes began to focus, she saw Meg's hand on her arm and Meg's face leaning in close to hers.

"What?" Hannah asked. "What is it?"

"I dreamed about Bruce." Meg's voice shook with tears. "I dreamed he was dead—"

"No, Meg, that's all it was—just a dream." Hannah automatically reached up to hug her. "He'll be back tomorrow—you'll see."

"He was barking, and I tried to find him, but when I did, he was just lying there not moving, and I realized he was dead. And then I woke up—" Meg's voice shook harder, and she knelt beside Hannah. "And someone was standing over me."

Hannah held her sister close and stroked her hair. She was glad for the darkness so Meg couldn't see the fear on her own face.

"Tell me about the someone you saw," she said calmly.

"I don't know." Meg shook her head. "Someone was just there. Standing over me. Watching me sleep."

"It must have been part of the dream, Meg. You probably weren't really awake yet, you know?" Hannah gave her a quick squeeze. "Did you get a look at who was there? In your dream, I mean?"

"He was tall—"

"You said he."

Meg nodded and wiped her nose. "Yes, he was tall . . . thin, I think. I couldn't see his face, and he was all distorted in the shadows and everything. But as I woke up and realized he was there, there was this . . . this light in his eyes. His eyes were glowing."

"Shh. Just a nightmare. That's all."

Hannah hugged Meg tight, but her own heart was exploding in her chest. She propped herself higher and, over Meg's shoulder, took a quick survey of the room. It was hard to distinguish anything at first in the dim firelight. As her eyes began to adjust, she could see the empty couch, covers thrown helter-skelter, pillows on the floor. The fireside, too, was deserted. She and Meg were alone in the room.

Hannah grabbed Meg's shoulders and held her back.

"Where's Jonathon? And Lance?"

"I don't know," Meg sniffled, glancing around nervously. "I thought they were here."

"What happened when you woke up and saw the man?" Hannah asked. "Did the dream just disappear?"

Meg shook her head. "It wasn't like that. I was so scared, I just stared at him, and he kind of stepped back into the shadows. And then just . . . you know . . . sort of faded away."

Hannah followed the direction of Meg's eyes. The chair she'd been sleeping in was near the door that led out to the hallway. In Meg's state of mind, anyone standing there could simply have stepped back through the door and vanished into the shadows beyond.

"You didn't hear anything?" Hannah persisted. "You didn't hear Lance or Jonathon leaving?"

"No." Meg sounded so sad that Hannah didn't pursue it.

"Go back to bed," she said. "Everything's okay."

*You're trying to convince yourself, but you don't believe that any more than Meg does—*

"Go on," Hannah coaxed. "Before you catch cold."

*It could have been Lance standing over Meg . . . Jonathon or Lance, either one. . . . They could have heard her crying in her sleep . . . they could have been checking on her to make sure she was okay. . . .*

"If anything's happened to Bruce—"

"Nothing has," Hannah insisted, forcing confidence into her voice. "We'll find him tomorrow. I'm sure he'll come home."

She waited till Meg climbed back into the chair and pulled the covers tight around her. She lay there listening till Meg's breathing became deep and regular. Then very carefully she got up and crept out into the hall.

*Where are they? Where could they have gone at this time of night? And why didn't we hear them?*

"Something's happened," Hannah mumbled to herself. "Something must have happened to them."

A thousand jolts of terror coursed through her. She gripped the wall and took several deep breaths to steady herself.

*Kurt. It must be Kurt. He's come back to finish the joke. . . .*

Hannah made her way slowly down the corridor, feeling along the wall. She was furious with herself for not grabbing a flashlight, but she just hadn't been thinking. She continued on toward the kitchen, when something suddenly made her freeze.

Hannah flattened herself against the wall.

*Footsteps? On the kitchen floor?*

She closed her eyes, ears straining through the horrible silence. It was a silence underscored by the shriek of the wind and the rattle of windowpanes, by the gusts through the cracks and the banging of outside shutters, by the creaking and groaning of old walls and warped floorboards and ancient foundations. It was a silence she thought she'd grown used to, except now, in her state of panic, it was suddenly deafening, and she wanted to scream.

Once more Hannah craned her head forward, trying to hear. Her hands clutched the wall, and still she was afraid to open her eyes.

The sounds came again . . . faint . . . fading.

Not old-house noises, she was sure of that now—not the old-house noises she heard every day, but something else. Something different.

*Something dangerous.*

She pressed harder against the wall.

*Where's Jonathon—where's Lance? Something's happened to them—I know it—I know it!*

Her mind raced feverishly. She needed a weapon—something to protect herself and Meg. A log maybe—there were some by the fireplace—or she could turn over one of the lanterns and take Meg and run. Better to lose their house than their lives—

A door creaked.

So softly that at first Hannah thought she'd only imagined it.

She took a step forward and held her breath.

She wondered why the sound didn't come again, and then slowly it dawned on her. *Someone's been in here, someone's been in the house, but now they've gone back outside.*

She hurried into the kitchen. She found the drawer in the counter and took out the flashlight. The room looked ghostly and strange around her ... a make-believe setting in a play that nobody ever really used.

Where were Jonathon and Lance?

Hannah went slowly to the window and peered out across the snowy landscape. The sheer desolation of their predicament hit her full force, and she quickly turned away, trembling.

*Where are they ... have they left us here?*

All this time she'd wanted them to go. And now that she couldn't find them ...

Hannah shook her head angrily. She wouldn't get hysterical; she had Meg and their survival to think of.

"Be reasonable," she muttered to herself. "Think!"

Nobody could have sneaked into the house and done anything to the guys without her or Meg hearing anything. After all, the four of them had been sleeping in close proximity in the same room. *And yet you didn't hear Meg get up at first—it took you a while to even realize she was talking to you.*

Hannah turned around and left the kitchen. Shining the light in front of her, she tiptoed up the stairs and down the hallway past the bedrooms. Lance had shut all the doors up here earlier. Now Hannah stood outside Meg's bedroom, remembering the teddy bear and the bent screen. She put her hand on the doorknob . . . hesitated . . . then quickly pushed it open.

Everything looked normal.

Breathing a sigh of relief, Hannah continued on down the hall, checking the other rooms. Everything was as it should have been, except she still couldn't find the guys. Fear was building steadily inside her—that sick taste of something gone terribly wrong that hadn't yet been discovered.

She wasn't sure why she decided to check Meg's room again.

She was almost past it when this insistent feeling gnawed at the back of her mind, and she opened the door one more time and went in.

And if the room hadn't been so dark, she probably wouldn't have seen the light at all, probably wouldn't even have noticed it glowing so strange, so ghostlike outside the window. . . .

Catching her breath, Hannah crossed the room and pressed in close to the frosted pane. She could see it now, pale and hazy, floating through the snow, iridescent as fog, weaving through the woods behind the house.

*A lantern?*

As Hannah watched in mounting fear, the light suddenly flickered and went out.

Everything lay still and silent as death.

"Someone's out there," Hannah whispered.

Someone who didn't want to be seen.

Someone who must have sensed she was watching.

And then a sound rose up . . . faint . . . mournful . . . far away.

It was a sound of pain . . . of dying.

And as Hannah listened to the unearthly howl, her skin crawled and her blood turned to ice in her veins.

She ran back downstairs and dived into her sleeping bag, and then she lay there trembling, eyes wide with fear.

She couldn't tell Meg what she'd just seen upstairs . . .

Or especially what she'd just heard.

*It's just a coyote,* she argued with herself. *A coyote or a wild dog—some mangy stray—some stupid animal caught in some stupid trap . . .*

But for one horrible second, it had sounded just like Bruce.

# 20

Hannah didn't even realize she slept.

The last thing she remembered was lying there crying, her head buried in her arms, so Meg wouldn't hear.

The sounds of the agonized howl ran through her mind again and again till she thought she'd start screaming herself. The house loomed over and around her, cold and dark and threatening.

*They've left us,* she thought, and her mind was slipping away, mercifully, into deep, deep oblivion, so that she didn't have to think anymore, didn't have to think what to do—*Lance and Jonathon have left Meg and me here alone and our time's running out. . . .*

"She's still sleeping. She must be worn-out."

Hannah could hear voices, but somehow they wouldn't compute. She groaned and turned onto her side, yet the voices came again, cutting rudely through the blessed numbness of sleep.

"You better wake her up."

"Okay. As soon as I finish."

She opened her eyes. Her head ached, and her face felt swollen from crying. Jonathon was standing by the couch, getting dressed. His jeans were zipped, but not buttoned, slung low on his hips. He was pulling a T-shirt on over his head, and he was barefoot. He stood slightly angled on his good leg, and his movements were very slow. Hannah groaned and pulled the blanket over her head.

"Don't look at me. I'm a mess."

She could hear the smile in his voice. "Hardly that. Come on. It's morning."

And then it came back to her, hitting her with such force that she forgot her swollen eyes and sat upright and stared at him.

"Jonathon!"

He seemed startled. He pulled his T-shirt the rest of the way down and gave a hesitant nod, as if not quite sure of his own identity.

"Where were you last night?" Hannah demanded.

"Why . . ." He looked puzzled. "I was here."

Hannah glared at him. "Don't lie to me!"

She flung off the covers and got to her knees, running one hand back through her tangled hair. She felt rumpled and dirty, and she knew she needed makeup and a toothbrush—and she was suddenly so miserable and so furious and so tired of being confused and afraid that she shoved him.

She didn't realize he'd just started to take a step.

As Hannah's blow made contact, a look of surprise went over Jonathon's face. Caught totally off guard and off balance, he staggered sideways and, with a look of sheer anguish, rammed into one corner of the couch.

For a second Hannah thought he might pass out.

His face went stark white, and as he grabbed for something to hold on to, he stumbled and nearly fell.

Hannah stared at him in total horror, unable to believe what she'd done.

"Oh, my God," she murmured, and she was on her feet, reaching for him, trying to pull him up straight, while all the time Jonathon kept leaning away from her arms.

"No," he gasped. "No, don't."

"Oh, I'm so sorry—Jonathon, really—I can't believe I did that—"

And she was vaguely aware of movement behind her, and suddenly Lance and Meg were there, too, everyone talking at once, everyone reaching for Jonathon, who was just as frantically trying to avoid all physical contact.

"What happened?" Lance said tightly.

He was gazing at Jonathon's leg, and Hannah could see the blood seeping through Jonathon's pants. Instinctively Jonathon put his hand down to cover it, and his fingers came back red and sticky.

"What the hell have you done?" Lance glared at Hannah, and his eyes flashed with a fierce light. Hannah shook her head and backed away.

"I'm so sorry—I didn't realize—I didn't mean—"

"Don't touch—" Jonathon began again, but Lance ignored him and forced him down onto the couch.

"You've torn the stitches open," Lance said, and the look he gave Hannah was positively lethal. "I'll have to sew him up all over again."

Hannah looked desperately from one accusing face to another. And then suddenly her anger and frustration boiled up again and spilled out.

"I didn't do it on purpose!" she shouted. "You act like I did it on purpose!"

"You did do it on purpose," Jonathon mumbled, and Hannah fought back sudden tears.

"Well, where were you last night?" she demanded. "When Meg had a nightmare and saw someone in the house—and there were footsteps and that light in the woods and the—" She broke off, not wanting to say anything about the howl, but not knowing how to get out of it now. "And the horrible noise—some wild animal, probably—"

They were all staring at her.

As Hannah ran out of words and focused in on their faces, it came to her suddenly that they all thought she'd totally lost her mind.

"I didn't imagine it," she said fiercely.

Nobody spoke. Everyone kept staring.

"Someone came in while Meg was sleeping!" she insisted. "Meg saw him!"

"You told me I was dreaming." Meg frowned.

Hannah searched desperately for words. "Well . . . well, Meg and I were all alone in the house—I know I wasn't dreaming that—"

"I went out to get wood once," Lance said. "So the fire wouldn't go out."

"And I was up once to use the bathroom," Jonathon added.

"Both of us would have had to pass by Meg's chair," Lance pointed out.

Hannah looked back at three pairs of eyes.

"I'm not the crazy one here," she muttered.

"No," Lance said dryly. "Just sadistic."

To Hannah's horror she felt tears brimming in her eyes—hot tears of anger and fear and shame. She opened her mouth to apologize again, but nothing came out. Abruptly she turned on her heel and left the room.

*Getting wood . . . using the bathroom . . . having nightmares . . . Well, you woke up this morning, didn't you? Still very much alive? No Kurt, no escaped killer—*

*Maybe Meg wasn't the one dreaming,* Hannah thought miserably, *maybe I was the one having all the nightmares. Maybe I just dreamed I went upstairs . . . saw the light in the woods . . . heard that animal howling. Maybe I just imagined I heard footsteps in the kitchen. . . .*

She went up to her room and shut the door behind her. She didn't care that the room was unbearably cold—in fact, she welcomed it.

*I'll shower and change. That'll put things back in perspective.*

She undressed quickly, welcoming the icy shock against her bare skin. She got in the shower and turned it on and realized too late there was no hot water. *Great. What else can happen?* She washed in record time and wrapped herself in a big robe, and then she sat down on the edge of her bed and felt sorry for herself.

*What have I done? I might have crippled Jonathon for life.*

This time she did let the tears come. She cried and cried till there were no more tears left, and then she rummaged dejectedly through her closet for clean clothes. She took off her robe and wriggled slowly into her jeans and sweater. She turned around and saw Lance standing in her doorway.

"What are you *doing!*" She jumped back, her face flaming. "Don't you know anything about knocking!"

"The door was open," he said blandly.

"The door was not open!" she threw back at him. "How dare you just come in and—"

"Relax," Lance sighed. "I just got here; I didn't see a thing. And the door was *open.*"

"You were watching me!"

"Watching you?" Lance said slowly, as if considering the possibility. "If *that* was on my mind, a locked door wouldn't do you much good."

Hannah's face went even redder. She grabbed another sweater and crammed it down over her head. She started past him, but he grabbed her arm and stopped her in her tracks.

"Okay." He nodded. "What about the footsteps you heard last night? That light you saw?"

For a second Hannah stared at him in surprise. Then her look turned defensive.

"Why bother?" she grumbled. "You won't believe me anyway."

"I believe you," Lance said simply. "But I don't want to talk in front of Meg. And I don't need Jonathon feeling like he has to play hero and start defending everyone. He can hardly stand up as it is."

The reminder hurt. Hannah turned away from him and walked slowly to the window.

"I was so mad," she sighed. "I wanted to take it out on someone . . . but I never meant to hurt Jonathon."

A silence hung between them.

"He knows that," Lance said at last.

"Do you?"

"Does it matter?"

Hannah shrugged.

"Look . . ." Lance relented. "He's stitched up again, okay? Just a few. It wasn't as bad as it looked."

Hannah's glance was suspicious. "Really?"

"Really."

Nodding slowly, she stared out across the backyard, and then she told him her story.

She told him about Meg's dream and what she'd heard in the kitchen. She told him about the light through the trees, and how unnervingly familiar that howl had sounded in the night. When she finished, Lance was gazing down at the floor.

"So," he said. "That's it?"

Hannah stared at him. "What do you mean, is that it? Isn't that enough?"

"Enough for what? Enough for you to think your boyfriend's still out there somewhere on a mad rampage?"

Hannah couldn't believe what she was hearing. "Wait. Just a minute ago, you said you *believed* me."

"I do believe you. I believe you really saw and heard those things. But they were"—Lance raised his eyebrow—"just things."

Hannah opened her mouth to protest, but he went on.

"Noises in the house . . . some nightmare Meg had . . . the wind howling . . ."

Hannah drew herself up indignantly. "You can't explain those things away like that! And what about the light I saw through the trees—"

173

"I told you I went out for wood," Lance said smoothly. "I took a flashlight with me. It was probably just a reflection through the snow."

"That was no reflection!"

"Everything has a logical explanation. Jonathon and I were both gone for a little while—Meg probably saw us by her chair and worked it into her dream. You've been worried about Bruce, so that's what you thought of when the wind was howling—"

"It was more than that."

"Look, everyone's cooped up and on edge—"

"Don't patronize me! I know what I heard. *And* saw!"

"It's bound to happen under the circumstances, but let's not make it worse, okay?"

Hannah boldly met his eyes. "Why don't you want anyone else to know about this?"

"Because I don't want to start a panic attack." His answer was immediate and matter-of-fact. "I don't want minds blowing or nerves snapping." A muscle clenched in his jaw, and he fixed her with a narrowed stare. "And I especially don't want another little accident happening like the one we just went through downstairs."

Hannah was so angry, she was shaking. She shoved past him and went down to the living room. Jonathon was slumped in a chair, staring vacantly out the window. Hannah could see Meg outside, bundled up and trudging across the yard.

"Where's she going?" Hannah asked.

"She's really upset about Bruce," Jonathon answered. "She's going to look for him."

Hannah flung open the front door and yelled for Meg to come back. If Meg heard, she gave no sign.

Instead she kept on doggedly through the snow, heading off toward the tree line that bordered the left side of the house.

"She shouldn't go out there alone," Hannah fretted, and Jonathon gave her a grim smile.

"Right. Just let me run out and bring her back."

His face was ashen. Hannah looked down at him and felt her heart twist painfully in her chest.

"Jonathon . . . I don't know what to say. I'm just so sorry—I lost my temper—I—"

Before she could finish, Lance came into the room, shrugging into his jacket, squinting through the window.

"What's she doing out there?" He frowned. "I told her to wait, and I'd help her look for him."

"I'll go with her," Hannah said quickly, but from the look Lance gave her, she might as well have been a bothersome fly.

"I have to go anyway," he replied smoothly. "I need to bring more wood up from the pile. We're going through it too fast."

Hannah hurried to the kitchen to get her coat. By the time she got back to the living room again, Lance already had the door open and was saying something to Jonathon. As Hannah started to go out, he put up his arm to block her way.

"I'll go with Meg," he said evenly. "See if you can find any more painkillers for Jonathon. And don't let him move around. Tie him to the couch if you have to."

Hannah nodded. She couldn't even look at Jonathon. Instead she kept her eyes on Meg, who was rapidly disappearing down the slope of the hill in front of the house.

"I don't want her getting lost," she mumbled. "It'd be just like her to wander off and not be able to find her way back."

"Well, we both know she'll listen to me before she will you." Lance turned up the collar on his jacket and ran a hand back through his hair. His eyes flicked briefly to Hannah's face, then shifted to Meg's distant figure. "Don't worry. I won't let her out of my sight."

Hannah suppressed a shiver. She went back into the living room and paced nervously from one end to the other. Jonathon, too, seemed peculiarly agitated. She watched for a while as he kept fidgeting and changing position on the couch, then finally she stepped in front of him and put her hands on her hips.

"Will you please stay still?" she scolded him. "You're only making it worse."

"Sorry." He tried to smile, but what came out was too quick and much too strained. "I can't get comfortable."

"You've got to keep quiet—otherwise you'll break the stitches again."

She smoothed the covers around him. His face was like a tight, white mask, and Hannah eased down beside him.

"Don't be brave," she finally blurted out. "I can't stand it."

"I'm not being brave." Jonathon's look was helplessly frustrated. "And *I* can't stand it either."

They stared at each other. Then suddenly Jonathon began to chuckle. For a few seconds Hannah stared at him in amazement, then slowly, reluctantly, she gave in and smiled.

"Jonathon, this is definitely not funny." She shook

her head at him. "I feel horrible. Guilty and just . . . just . . ."

"You've been under a lot of strain," he said quietly. "I'm not blaming you for what happened. I just happened to be in the wrong place at the wrong time."

"Like the bridge," Hannah said dryly, and after a moment's thought, he nodded.

"Yes. Like the bridge."

"There're a million different places you could have ended up," Hannah went on miserably. "But you ended up here."

"I'm not complaining."

Hannah stared at him, his statement sinking in. And it suddenly occurred to her that she really hadn't heard him complain the whole time he'd been here, even with all that had happened to him.

"How do you do that?" she murmured, and he glanced at her in dismay.

"Do what?"

"Not complain."

Her question seemed to surprise him. "I complain," he said.

"When?"

"Lots of times."

"I've never heard you."

"You haven't been around me that much."

"That's true—"

"And you don't know me that well."

Again Hannah mulled over his words. "Don't I?" she said at last, and Jonathon glanced at her, shaking his head.

"I didn't mean to sound so mysterious. Actually, I'm pretty shallow."

Hannah stared at him. His head was tilted back against the cushions, and lines of pain were working around the corners of his mouth. His hair looked silky . . . soft . . . falling stubbornly over his forehead . . . curling damply from the sweat on his brow.

Slowly Hannah reached over. She put her palm against his forehead and gently smoothed his hair back from his face.

He wasn't expecting it. He turned his head to look at her, and somewhere far back beneath all the pain, Hannah could see a tiny flicker of surprise. It made him look vulnerable, Hannah thought, and almost shy, and as she gazed back at him, she felt herself lean forward and kiss him lightly on the lips.

Jonathon's arm came up behind her.

It slipped gently around her shoulders and drew her close.

They kissed again, harder this time, and then again, and Hannah could feel the race of their heartbeats, the harsh, quick catch of their breathing—both his arms around her now as she leaned into him and he held her, down, down into the cushions, his touch so light, so careful, fingertips over her cheeks, her hair, even as she felt him flinch in pain, not wanting her to know, not wanting her to hear his moan, as faint as a single breath. . . .

"I'm hurting your leg," Hannah said unhappily. She pulled away from him, frowning down at his bravely composed face. "I'm sorry. I didn't mean to."

Jonathon shook his head. "You didn't."

"The thing is," Hannah went on, standing up now, crossing to the fireplace, "I don't know why I did that. It's not the kind of thing I usually do. I—" She laced her fingers together, stammering, "Well, what I mean is, I don't want you to think that I just—"

Frustrated, she broke off. Jonathon was propped up on one elbow watching her, a smile playing at the corners of his mouth. He looked like he was enjoying himself immensely.

"It's my fault, about your leg," Hannah burst out. "But that's not why I did what I just did—I mean, I'm *sorry* about your leg, but that didn't have anything to do with—I wouldn't have—"

"I believe you." Jonathon nodded, deadpan. "And you're putting it so well."

Flustered, Hannah headed for the door, but he caught her arm and stopped her as she went by.

"You don't have to explain to me why you do or don't do things, okay?" Jonathon said gently, looking up into her face. "I'm not Kurt, Hannah. You don't need my permission—or my approval—to be yourself."

Hannah stared at him in confusion. For one second an image of Kurt rose up in her mind, and all the fear, the anger, the indignation, came back in a rush. With an effort, she made herself focus on Jonathon. *His eyes . . . his touch . . . his kiss . . .*

"Kurt's always reminding me how much I hurt him," she mumbled at last. "How much I mess up his life when I don't agree with what he says or does. When things don't go his way, it's always my fault. . . ."

She tried to make it sound like a joke, but the words came out empty. She glanced reluctantly at Jonathon's face . . . at the bloody stain on his jeans.

"I don't want to hurt you," she whispered.

For a long moment Jonathon gazed back at her.
He lifted one hand to her face . . .
Touched it gently against her cheek.
"Hurt me?" he murmured.
And he smiled.
"I'll never let you, Hannah. I'll never let you hurt me."

# 21

Without warning, the front door flew open.

Hannah jumped back from the couch as Meg and Lance came into the room. With a quick, telltale gesture she tried to smooth back her hair, then caught the knowing look Lance threw her. Her cheeks grew warm, and she quickly glanced away.

"We can't find him, Hannah," Meg said miserably, going over to the fire. She held her hands out to the flames, and tears glistened on her cheeks. "We can't find him anywhere. I think something's really happened to him."

*The howling . . . only the wind . . . remember what Lance told you . . . only the wind—*

"We'll find him," Hannah said firmly. "He probably just doesn't want to come home yet."

"But we've looked in all his favorite places." Meg's voice broke. "We've looked . . . and looked . . ."

"We'll all look," Jonathon spoke up suddenly. "There's got to be someplace we haven't thought of."

"You're not looking for anything," Lance reminded him, but Jonathon pointedly ignored the comment.

"We can split up," Jonathon insisted. "We'll cover more ground that way." Gritting his teeth, he tried to get up from the couch. He pushed himself into a sitting position and stayed there.

"You're not going anywhere." Lance pushed him down again. "Are you crazy?"

"And you hold it, too, Meg," Hannah ordered as Meg started for the door. "You're half-frozen as it is."

"But, Hannah, I've *got* to go! Bruce'll *come* to me—"

"No, Hannah's right," Lance said solemnly. "Bruce can't hear you call him anyway. And if he *does* come back while we're gone, someone should be here to let him in and take care of him."

"I can still go with you." Again Jonathon tried to get up; again Lance pushed him down.

"Someone's got to stay with Meg," Hannah argued. She put on her jacket and motioned toward the window. "What if Kurt's still out there somewhere? I don't want Meg alone in the house."

Lance and Jonathon exchanged looks.

At last Jonathon gave a sigh and eased back carefully on the couch. "Okay, fine, sure," he grumbled. "I'll stay."

"Well, then," Lance said, raising an eyebrow at Hannah. "I guess that leaves you and me."

Something about the way he said it . . .

For one brief instant Hannah felt a stab of fear. She saw a second look pass between Lance and Jonathon, and then Lance was opening the door.

Meg went over and took hold of his arm. "Please," she begged, "promise you'll find him."

"Meg . . ." Hannah paused, zipping up her jacket. "You know he can't promise—"

"I'll *find* him," Lance said. He gave Meg a curt nod, then went out the door, leaving Hannah open-mouthed.

"You shouldn't have told her that!" Hannah fumed, following him across the yard. "If you *don't* find him, Meg's never going to forgive either one of us."

"You take the woods on the other side of the road," Lance directed. "I'll search the higher ground behind the house, then meet you in front."

Hannah looked back at the porch. She could see Meg in the window, and she lifted her hand to wave. A feeling of dread fluttered in the pit of her stomach—a feeling that was growing stronger every second.

*What's wrong with you? Jonathon's right in there with her. . . .*

But with that bad leg of his, he'd be even more helpless than Meg. . . .

Hannah watched Lance walk back to the tree line. For a split second he hesitated, but then he stepped through and disappeared, as though the woods had swallowed him whole. She stood for a moment looking at the spot where he'd been. What if he didn't come out again? What if he simply disappeared like Bruce?

The doghouse, she thought suddenly. With all that had happened, had anyone even bothered to check Bruce's doghouse?

She could see it from here—a snowy little igloo stuck far back in a clump of oak trees. She couldn't even tell if Bruce had used it recently—the yard was crisscrossed with so many footprints now, all shifted and shaken and faded by the wind and snow, that it was impossible to tell which tracks went with what.

"You stupid dog," she groaned. "Where *are* you?"

She couldn't even stand to think about Meg without Bruce. She squared her shoulders and plowed toward the doghouse, and the thought came to her suddenly —how funny it would be to find Bruce fast asleep, totally oblivious to all the tears and trouble he'd caused—

Hannah stopped, frowning.

Drifts practically hid the doghouse entrance, but something had managed to work its way through anyway, leaving a sort of trough between chunks of snow and ice.

Slowly Hannah leaned down.

She took a cautious step toward the opening and squinted into the darkness.

"Bruce?"

She could smell the cold . . . the thick layer of straw, damp now where snow had blown in.

"Bruce? Are you in here?"

She could even smell Bruce's old blanket . . . the furry, dusty scent of him still muffled in old wool . . .

And something else . . .

Something stronger than the cold . . . something sharp and metallic that made her feel light-headed . . . queasy . . .

And suddenly she didn't want to see inside, didn't want to see what was in there, and she had to get Lance, she'd make Lance look in the doghouse—

Hannah took off across the yard.

She shouted Lance's name, but he didn't answer.

Stopping at the edge of the woods, she called again, but her own voice echoed back, taunting her. For just a split instant, she thought she'd seen someone standing beside the house close to the driveway. A tall dark figure against the snow . . . but when she blinked and looked around, he was gone.

In growing panic, Hannah swung back around, then screamed as a sudden movement caught her eye.

*Lance?*

Then why wouldn't he answer her?

She ran to the road in front. As far as she could see, there were no signs that anyone had come this way. Thoroughly shaken, she stood there and tried to reason with herself.

*I guess I imagined it. . . . I must have imagined someone—something—in the snow. . . .*

And then it dawned on her—maybe Lance had seen someone, too—maybe he was cutting through the woods even now, trying to warn her without being heard.

*I've got to tell Jonathon—*

Hannah turned and started back. She'd gone only a few feet when she heard the screams.

*Meg!*

Hannah raced for the house. She could hear Meg screaming and screaming, and a thousand images stabbed through her—*the killer—Kurt—Bruce dead* —and as she finally cleared the yard and hurtled up the steps, she saw Meg run out onto the porch, sobbing hysterically.

"What is it!" Hannah shouted, but she couldn't understand, Meg babbling incoherently as she collapsed in Hannah's arms. "What is it?" Hannah shook her. "Stop it, Meg—tell me what's wrong!"

"The window!" Meg wailed. "He was there! He was *there!*"

"Who was? Calm down and talk to me, Meg. *Who!*"

"A face!" Meg sobbed. "He was looking in at me and—and—he had an *axe!*"

# 22

Somehow Hannah managed to get Meg inside and lock the door.

"Jonathon!" she shouted, running into the hall. *"Jonathon!"*

"He's not here," Meg whimpered.

"Not here? What do you mean, he's not here—"

"He heard noises outside. He went out to see what they were—"

"Jonathon!"

Hannah flew down the hall to the kitchen. The back door was standing open, and as she got to it, Jonathon pushed it from outside. Hannah yanked it open, and he practically fell on the floor.

"What do you think you're doing, leaving her alone like that!" Hannah railed at him. "You were supposed to stay with her!"

Jonathon looked totally bewildered. "Well . . . I *did* stay. I *am* here with—"

"You went outside! And while you were gone, someone looked in the window at her!"

"The . . . window?" He sounded stunned. "Are you—are you sure?"

They both turned as Meg came into the room. Her eyes filled her narrow face.

"I'm sure!" Meg insisted. "He was there! I saw him!"

"What'd he look like?" Jonathon asked, and Meg shook her head in confusion.

"I don't know. I mean, I'm not sure! I mean, he had a ski mask on, so I couldn't see his face."

Hannah caught her breath. The room seemed to close in on her with a dizzying spin, and then it slowly settled back into focus.

"A . . . ski mask?" Jonathon coaxed, and again Meg nodded.

"It came down over his head. I just saw his eyes. They were . . . horrible."

"But you couldn't see anything else?" Jonathon asked carefully. "What color his eyes were, could you tell that?"

"Dark. Everything was dark."

"The mask was dark?"

"Black, I think. Yes . . . I think . . . black."

*Kurt*, Hannah thought automatically. *Kurt has a black ski mask.*

"Lots of people wear black ski masks," Jonathon said, as if reading her mind. "It could have been anyone." He hesitated, then offered cautiously, "Or . . you know . . . nobody. She could have seen a shadow or something."

"She didn't see a shadow," Hannah snapped at

him. "*I* saw something in the driveway when I was outside a while ago. And don't tell me *I* imagined it."

Jonathon was looking more baffled by the minute. "What'd you see?"

"I don't know—what difference does it make!" Hannah's voice rose. "Something! A person!"

"Are you sure? Where was he?"

"Outside by the driveway! By the house! It had to have been the same person Meg saw at the window!"

"Look!" Meg choked.

As they all three stared at the door, the knob slowly began to turn.

"Lock it," Meg whispered, "lock it—lock it—"

Hannah saw Jonathon's hand reaching out . . . saw his fingers stretched toward the bolt. With a crash the door flew back against the wall, and the girls shrieked in terror.

"Jesus, Lance." Jonathon put one hand to his heart and sagged against the wall as Lance froze in the doorway and stared back at them.

"What?" Lance demanded.

Hannah couldn't even talk. For one quick second she realized how much he resembled the figure she'd seen outside—tall, black silhouette, black shadowy features. . . .

"Did you notice anything outside?" Jonathon asked, and at Lance's bewildered expression, added, "Meg saw someone looking in the window."

"The window?" Lance frowned.

"Footprints!" Hannah exclaimed suddenly. "He had to have left footprints! They wouldn't be gone this fast, right?"

She started outside, but Meg grabbed her.

"No! Don't go out there!"

For a moment Jonathon and Hannah locked eyes.

"I never should have left her," Jonathon murmured, but Hannah was already following Lance outside.

"There they are!" Hannah motioned triumphantly as she spotted faint indentations beneath the window.

"What's left of them." Lance's tone was solemn. He squatted down and peered close to the ground.

"Just like the woodpile," Hannah mumbled.

Lance looked at her sharply. "What?"

"The woodpile. Earlier I saw tracks by the woodpile, but they were all messed up. Like someone deliberately tried to wipe them out."

Now she gazed down at the thick, white ground. Where fading prints remained, the snow around them was rough and unsettled.

"Maybe," Lance mumbled. "But the wind could have done it, too. They could even be mine."

Hannah turned on him in surprise. "What do you mean?"

"I came this way around the house a few times, looking for Bruce. Checking the bushes. Look, you and I have been all over this yard. There are prints *everywhere*. And if Jonathon was out here, too . . ."

Hannah's heart fell. "Were you close to the house?"

He nodded.

"It could have been you, then," she said tightly. "It could have been you *or* Jonathon—you could have been trying to scare her."

Lance look annoyed. "Or Kurt," he said dryly. "And by all means, don't forget that escaped killer."

Hannah turned and went back inside. Meg looked up from her chair as Hannah slipped out of her coat

"Did you find anything?" she asked hopefully, but Hannah shook her head.

"There were footprints by the window, all right," she said glumly. "From everyone and his brother." When Meg slumped unhappily, Hannah ventured, "Meg . . . are you absolutely *sure* you saw something?"

"Don't you believe me?" To Hannah's surprise, Meg jumped to her feet. "What's the matter with you? Bruce is gone, and I saw someone at the window! *Why doesn't anyone believe me?*"

"We believe you," Jonathon assured her. "Look . . . we're all under a lot of strain and—"

"Well, we wouldn't be if you two hadn't shown up!" Hannah burst out.

"It's not their fault!" Meg protested, motioning to Jonathon's leg. "I'm sure he didn't tear his leg open just for the fun of it!"

"Maybe he did." Lance shrugged, pausing in the doorway. "Some murderers really enjoy pain."

"That's so sick." Hannah turned on him. "That's so—"

"Calm down!" Jonathon's voice rose, and everyone went quiet. "We're not going to solve anything this way. Look . . . it was wrong of me to go off and leave Meg by herself, okay? From now on I'll stay right here with her. But the first thing we have to do is find Bruce. We're just wasting time arguing when we should be looking for him."

"He's right," Meg said, her voice breaking. "He might be out there *dying!* And you're all just—"

"Oh, Meg." Hannah grabbed her and hugged her. "Meg, shh. I'm sorry—we're *all* sorry. Come on now,

Bruce isn't dying, and we'll find him, okay? We *will*. Lance and I'll go back out there right now and . . ."

Her voice trailed away as she remembered the doghouse; in all the excitement she'd forgotten about the strange smell. She stiffened slowly, casting a look at Lance, marveling at his powers of perception, for he already had the door open and was nodding at her as he started out again.

Meg sniffled and sat down on the hearth. She looked up at Hannah and shook her head.

"What's happening, Han? Everything's all wrong."

*What can I say?* Hannah paused, then forced a smile. "It seems that way now, but when the snow stops . . . you'll see. We'll find Bruce. . . ."

But they didn't find Bruce.

"It's blood, all right," Lance muttered as Hannah paced behind him at the doghouse. She could hardly bring herself to ask.

"Is he . . ."

"No." Lance crawled out again, his face grim. "He's not in there. But wherever that came from . . . there's a lot of it."

Hannah felt weak—from relief and a whole new set of fears.

They spent another half hour combing the surrounding woods and fields, but there was no sign of Bruce. Sick at heart, Hannah followed Lance back to the house, dreading what they'd tell Meg. But one look at their faces gave Meg the story, and she retreated to a corner and stared despondently at the wall.

For the second night, they ate and slept by the fire. Hannah talked Meg into making hamburgers, but nobody seemed hungry. No one had much to say. The wind howled around the house, and they kept the heaters burning, and an uneasy silence fell as they all curled up in their makeshift beds to try and sleep.

Jonathon insisted Meg take the couch. He slept on the floor near Lance, while Hannah stretched out beside the couch, where she could stay close to Meg.

Hannah lay awake for what seemed hours, a feeling of doom in her heart. It was almost as though some sixth sense had come into play . . . putting her on guard . . . waiting. But waiting for what?

When she finally did drift off, it was to strange and troubled dreams. She saw herself upstairs in bed, and Meg was trying to wake her up, terrified, and "Someone's at the door!" Meg kept saying over and over again. "Hannah, someone's at the door—" And "Go away!" Hannah screamed, but someone kept knocking and knocking, and she thought she'd die of fright—

She sat up with a cry. She was shaking all over and wet with sweat. She didn't know how long she'd been asleep.

*Did I really scream . . . or was that in my nightmare?*

But the knocking . . .

The knocking had seemed so real. . . .

She heard Meg crying.

Frightened, Hannah felt along the couch, but it was empty. Following the sounds to the kitchen, she found her sister leaning on the counter, staring out into the falling snow.

"Meg?" Hannah whispered.

She expected Meg to be sleepwalking . . . caught in the twilight zone of some personal nightmare of her own. So it surprised her when she heard Meg's voice.

"Did you hear it, Hannah?" Meg mumbled.

"Hear what?"

"Those sounds."

Hannah listened. She didn't hear anything.

"What are you doing up?" she asked.

"Following you."

"Me?" Hannah's skin crawled as Meg went on.

"I woke up, and you were in the hall. Well . . . I *thought* it was you. You said my name. You said, 'Meg, come with me. . . .' So I did."

Hannah's blood went cold. She shook her head slowly. Meg sounded very faraway.

"I saw your shadow come in here. I've been in here ever since."

Hannah took her arm. "Come back to bed now, Meg."

"But didn't you hear them?" Meg asked again. "You must have heard—"

"Where are the boys, Meg? Jonathon and Lance?"

Meg shrugged her shoulders. "I don't know. Maybe they heard the sounds, too."

"Meg . . . what *sounds?*"

"You know," Meg murmured. "Like . . . chopping."

# 23

Hannah lay stiffly in her sleeping bag, not moving, not wanting to wake up Meg. She'd finally coaxed her back to the couch, and now she could hear the deep breathing of her sleep. The room was quiet save for that and the hiss and crackle of the fire. Hannah stared at the sputtering shadows along the walls and recalled Meg's words for the hundredth time.

*"You said my name . . . 'Meg, come with me. . . .'"*

*"Like . . . chopping."*

How much time had passed since then? Hannah didn't know. She strained her ears through the dark, and she waited.

*Where are they?*

She hadn't heard them get up . . . hadn't heard them leave the room. Were they still in the house somewhere, or had they gone outside? A slow, cold chill crept through her. She thought of the man at the window . . . the dark silhouette beside the driveway . . . Kurt's abandoned car . . . the missing axe . . .

*Bruce* . . .

Hannah buried her face against her pillow and fought back tears.

With every hour that went by, the chances of finding him alive got smaller and smaller.

*Where are they?*

That horrible sense of something very, very wrong came back full strength, paralyzing her. What possible reason would the guys have for both being gone in the middle of the night?

Then suddenly she heard the slow groan of the kitchen door.

*Jonathon? Lance?*

She opened her mouth to call out, but the words froze in her throat.

Suppose it wasn't them . . . suppose it was the man at the window or the figure beside the house . . . suppose it was Kurt or the murderer or—

Her heart nearly exploded.

Footsteps came through the kitchen . . . along the hallway. Slow and measured. Like footsteps not meant to be heard.

Meg moaned in her sleep, and Hannah realized she was squeezing her own blankets for dear life, gazing out beneath half-shut eyes. The doorway filled and grew dark. Someone stood there, looking in.

"It's okay," came a whisper. "They're still asleep."

Now two shadows moved cautiously across the room and eased down in front of the fire.

Hannah shook uncontrollably. Meg shifted and moaned again.

"They didn't hear it," another voice whispered.

Hannah heard the long slow stretching out of bodies on the floor . . . the low rustle of blankets being pulled into place. . . .

The room grew silent.

But still she lay there shivering, a premonition of tragedy pounding in her heart.

# 24

"Look, Hannah," Meg said. "There's a snowman outside."

Hannah jerked awake. She'd been having a dream about Bruce, but she couldn't remember what it was. Now she sat up, rubbing the stiffness from her arms, and looked over to where Meg stood beside the window peering out.

"Where's Jonathon?" Hannah mumbled. "Where's Lance?"

Meg shrugged. She sounded hoarse, like she might be getting a cold. "I don't know. I just woke up."

Stretching again, Hannah got to her feet. The floor was empty—sleeping bags and blankets folded neatly in a pile.

"That snowman," Meg mumbled again. "It's really big!"

"Let me see."

Pushing in beside her, Hannah gazed off across the

front yard. The snow was still falling, though not quite so thickly now, and a fine white fog hung over everything.

"It must be six feet tall," Meg said in awe. "And look . . . it sort of has an expression on its face."

Hannah nodded slowly, an eerie coldness going through her. The snowman stood facing the house, as if keeping a silent vigil. Its black eyes stared sightlessly, yet she had the weirdest feeling they could actually see. Its mouth was a round black circle, frozen in a silent cry.

Hannah murmured, "Close the curtains, Meg."

"I don't know, I think it's kind of funny," Meg countered. "Maybe they thought it would cheer us up."

Almost at once they heard the kitchen door open and the boys coming in. Hannah went to meet them, watching as Jonathon limped slowly to the table to hang his jacket on a chair. Lance tossed his onto the table.

"Nice touch," Hannah said dryly, and they both stared at her.

"What?" Jonathon finally said.

"The snowman. You must have gotten up at the crack of dawn, right?"

The boys looked at each other. Then they looked at her.

"What snowman?" they chorused together.

Hannah had no patience this morning. "Come on, it's not funny. I'm glad you think there's all this time to play games when Bruce is still missing and—"

"Wait a minute." Jonathon held up his hands to ward off her anger. He seemed totally drained . . . almost dazed. "That's where we've been—in the woods looking for Bruce. What game are you talking about?"

"The front yard," she retorted. "And don't say you haven't seen it. I'm not in the mood."

Again a quick exchange of looks between the boys. Without a word, they followed Hannah to the living room. She jerked back the curtain, and the three of them peered off across the snowy lawn.

*"That* snowman," Hannah said.

Jonathon turned to Lance. Lance met his eyes just as steadily.

"Look familiar now?" Hannah snapped, but her heart was going cold, cold inside her—*I don't like this—the looks on their faces—something's wrong— wrong*—Terror roared through her, and she stepped away, letting the curtain fall back into place.

"Kurt did it," she mumbled, and her hands flew to her mouth, trying to hold back the scream resounding through her head. "Kurt did it, didn't he! *He* did it—he—"

She was staring at Lance. His eyes were narrowed, and she could see the suspicion there.

"Kurt?" Jonathon mumbled. "If Kurt's serious about terrorizing you, I'd think he'd be lots more creative than building a snowman."

Hannah glanced from one of them to the other. *But you were both gone last night—you thought I was asleep, but I heard you—both of you were outside—*

There was a sound behind them, and Meg came into the room, blowing her nose into a tissue.

"Great snowman." She tried to smile.

Both boys mumbled under their breath.

"Did you find Bruce?" Meg asked. As they shifted

uncomfortably and mumbled again, her bottom lip began to tremble.

"We'll get some coffee and go back out," Lance said gruffly.

Hannah trailed them back to the kitchen. Lance set water on to boil. Jonathon sank into a chair, his face the color of chalk.

"You shouldn't go out there again—" Lance began, but Jonathon's look was almost angry.

"I'm going."

Hannah looked around the group. Meg huddled by the doorway, coughing, looking so little, so young. Jonathon slumped in his chair, pale and weak. Lance stared down at the stove. His face was dark . . . thoughtful . . . ready to snap at the slightest provocation. . . .

*One by one. We're falling apart. One . . . by . . . one.*

"*I'm* going to look for Bruce," Meg announced, but Hannah's tone was stern.

"No, Meg, you're already catching cold. All we need now is for you to get pneumonia. I'll go."

Before anyone could stop her, Hannah bundled up and ran out of the house. She felt like she was going to explode—she had to get away. Taking deep gulps of air, she ran to the front yard and stopped beside the snowman. Her lungs burned in her chest, and her skin felt raw. She wanted to cry, to scream. She stood and stared up at the giant round head and shivered uncontrollably.

The snowman stared back.

Hannah walked around it, frowning. Its body was huge—three gigantic snowballs piled one on top of the other—and it had a massive head. Someone had stuck a shovel in its backside, the blade wedged down through the base of its body, the handle protruding upward, stiff and straight as a spine. There was something unsettling about that, though Hannah wasn't exactly sure why. She stepped away from it and took a good look at its face. Lumps of snow and wood chips—yet somehow, it still seemed to be watching her, with an awareness that was almost . . . *human*.

Strangely unnerved, Hannah took off down the driveway.

"Bruce!" she screamed. But she knew he couldn't hear her, she knew it, yet she shouted anyway, because the sound of her own voice came back to her strong and loud, and she needed to hear something besides those three other people she was trapped with—

*Trapped!*

She *had* to do something—but what? They'd freeze to death before they could ever find help. But if they stayed here, they were sure to die. No lights, no phone, no radio, no—

*Radio!*

Hannah nearly reeled from the heady feeling of excitement. Kurt's car was useless, but sometimes he carried his *portable* radio with him—especially if he was on his way to a weekend trip. *Why didn't I think of it before*—

She stopped and leaned her head against a tree, trying to calm her nerves, and when a hand clamped down on her arm, she jumped back with a shriek.

"It's me!" Jonathon said. "It's me!"

"Don't you realize what's happening?" Hannah shouted at him. She was out of control and she knew it, but she couldn't stop yelling, couldn't stop the worry and fear that had been building up inside her all this time—

"Don't you realize what he's doing to us! He's *playing* with us! He's *teasing* us with all these horrible things and he's closing in—he's—"

Jonathon grabbed her and shook her. Her words caught in her throat, and she stared up at him in surprise.

"What are you talking about?" Jonathon demanded. "Come on, Hannah, stop it right now!"

*"You* know—" She was struggling to breathe, trying to make him understand, and when he didn't answer, she fought to break out of his grasp. *"You* know—"

"I *don't* know!" He gave her a final shake, then clasped her to him, holding her tightly. "Hannah, come on, please stop. Nobody's going to do anything to you or to Meg as long as Lance and I are here—don't you see that by now?"

*But you were gone last night—either one of you could have done it—both of you could have done it—*

"Then why didn't you see Kurt out here last night prowling around the house?" she accused him. "Why didn't you see someone looking in the window at Meg?"

Jonathon opened his mouth . . . closed it again. He shrugged helplessly, taking a step back.

"It just—" He seemed to be searching for words. "It just—well, I'm sorry, okay? But you're still safe, aren't you? Nothing happened."

*"That* time!" Hannah nearly shouted at him again. "But what about *next* time?"

She headed across the yard, down to the road, toward Kurt's abandoned car.

"Hey!" Jonathon yelled. "Where are you going?"

"To get a radio!"

"But the battery's dead!"

Hannah got to Kurt's car and started digging through the drifts against the front door. After several minutes she heard Jonathon come up behind her, and together they started flinging snow away.

"Would you mind telling me why we're doing this?" Jonathon finally broke the silence, and Hannah cast him an impatient look.

"He might have brought a radio from home," she explained. "He was going out of town, and he might have put one in his car. Only I don't remember seeing one when I looked in here yesterday—" She bit her lip in frustration. "But I didn't really look in the backseat. He might have put it in the backseat—"

"Maybe you just didn't notice it. Don't give up yet."

At last they got enough snow clear, and Jonathon tugged on the door handle.

The door wouldn't move.

"Damn! It must have frozen shut last night!" Hannah moved in beside him and gave the door several good hard kicks. "Okay. Try it again."

Throwing her an admiring glance, Jonathon pulled again. This time the door came open, and Hannah crawled inside, searching along the seats and the floor.

"Nothing," she said tearfully. "There's nothing here."

"What about the trunk?" Jonathon asked. "Would he have packed it in the trunk?"

"Even if he did, we'll never get it open." Hannah took the hand he offered her and crawled out again.

"If we had a crowbar, maybe I could pry it."

"Really?" Hannah was almost afraid to hope. She took a long, careful look at Jonathon as he leaned against the car. She could tell he was shivering, though he made every effort to hide it from her, and lines of pain were etched deeply into every line of his face. "You wait here," she said. "I'll go get Lance and try to find something we can use."

"Hey, I'm not an invalid, you know." Indignantly Jonathon eased around to the back of the car. Hannah saw him stare down at the trunk and then run his fingers along the edges of the lid. He glanced at her and frowned.

"What's wrong?" Hannah asked.

"Weird. The crack feels wider than it should."

"Which means?"

"Which means maybe Kurt didn't shut it tight the last time he used it."

"But it's still frozen, right?"

"Right. But maybe we can hit it with something and unjam it."

Hannah brightened. "There's a big branch around here somewhere. I found it yesterday next to the door."

Jonathon nodded. He made his way back along the side of the car, leaving Hannah to stare at the trunk. She tried to slide her fingers beneath the lid, but they wouldn't go.

"Did you find it?" She could see Jonathon bending over, groping through drifts, his cheeks taut with pain. "It should be there by the driver's side."

"Not yet. I'll go back to the house and get something."

Hannah scarcely heard him. She balled up her fists

and beat all over the trunk. Her hands stung, and she swore under her breath, and then she beat on the trunk again.

Once more she worked her fingertips into the crack beneath the lid and pulled.

To her astonishment, she felt it give just a little.

"Jonathon?"

She pulled again, and the lid slowly began to open.

"Jonathon, I think I've got it!"

The first thing she saw was a heap of old blankets.

They were lumped and piled together at the bottom of the trunk, and Hannah reached in to rummage through them for the radio.

Her hand touched something cold and solid, and with a frown, she threw back the blankets to see what it was.

It was a face she recognized.

A face blue with cold . . . blue and cold and dead . . .

As Hannah screamed, someone grabbed her from behind.

She spun around and saw Jonathon looking past her into the trunk, his face blank with horror.

"Who—" he began, but Hannah fell against him.

"It's Ernie!" she cried. "Ernie Metzer—our bus driver!"

# 25

"Are—are you sure?" Jonathon whispered, and Hannah pulled back from him, her voice on the edge of hysteria.

"Of course I'm sure—do you think I can't recognize the guy who drives us back and forth to school five days a week! Oh my God—this can't be happening!"

Jonathon glanced around quickly—at the deserted road—the thick woods—the trees laced together with ice and snow.

"Come on," he said urgently. "Get back. Now! Back to the house!"

"Was it Kurt?" Hannah kept crying. Jonathon's arm was around her, steering her up the yard again, and she could feel his awkward gait, could feel him cringing in pain from the effort.

"I don't know," he mumbled. "Come on—hurry!"

207

"Ernie must have come to check on Meg and me—to see how we were—"

"Then where'd he come *from?* Where's his car?"

"How should I know?" Hannah's voice rose. "He could have parked miles from here and hiked in through the woods—he hated these back roads in snow like this!" She took a swipe at her wet cheeks. "He was so *nice*—so worried about us when he dropped us off the other day—"

"Don't think about that now."

"If Kurt saw Ernie hanging around the house, do you think he might have . . ." Hannah drew a deep breath, unable to finish the horrible speculation.

Jonathon's look was glum. "Thought Ernie was a boyfriend? Done away with the competition?"

"But he *knew* Ernie—he knew—"

"Maybe not. Maybe Kurt didn't get a good look at him. And if Kurt was in the state of mind you said he was—"

"What are we going to do about Ernie?"

"We have to leave him."

"We *can't* just leave him!"

"We can't bring him inside—we can't help him now, Hannah, he's dead!"

Hannah burst into fresh tears, but Jonathon relentlessly kept moving her toward the house.

"He must have been the one Meg saw at the window," Jonathon said. "It must have been him—"

"But he didn't have a ski mask! Meg said the guy had a ski mask—"

"It could have been in the trunk," Jonathon said grimly. "In his pocket—underneath him—maybe Kurt took it—"

"Or maybe *Kurt* was the one wearing the ski mask—"

"Quit talking about it. Just get in the house."

"You feel it, too, don't you? You feel it just like I do—that something terrible's going to happen to us—to *all* of us—"

"Dammit, Hannah, shut up about that, and go in the house!"

She swung at him, but he grabbed her hand. Pain shot across his face, and for one second he looked like he might pass out.

"I'm sorry," Hannah whispered, "I'm—"

"Just go," Jonathon said tightly. "And don't tell Meg."

Hannah ran ahead of him and started up the hill. She'd just reached the front yard when a scream cut through the stillness.

"Meg!" she gasped, then yelled, "Jonathon—come quick!"

She saw Lance on the porch and Meg silhouetted in the doorway. Lance was carrying something in his arms—something big and shapeless and black. . . .

"Oh, God," Hannah cried. *"Bruce!"*

By the time she got to the door, Lance was already inside. He was placing the dog gently on the rug before the fire, and Meg was standing behind him, wringing her hands and sobbing.

"He's dead—oh, Hannah . . . someone's killed Bruce—"

Hannah didn't dare answer. She was afraid she'd start screaming and never be able to stop. As Jonathon went to Lance, she watched Lance's long fingers go slowly over the dog's body. Bruce didn't appear to be breathing. His thick coat was matted with blood. As Lance looked up and shook his head, Jonathon's arms went slowly around Meg.

"No," Lance said softly, "he's not dead. But he's close to it."

"Where did you find him?" Hannah mumbled. "Where—"

"In the garage."

"But that's impossible—we looked in—"

"The garage." Lance cast her a dark look. "I know we looked there, but that's where he was."

Hannah bit off a reply. She could see the gash in Bruce's side, the gash that revealed flesh and bone beneath. She turned away and tightly shut her eyes.

"What happened to him?" Meg could hardly get the words out. "Oh, Hannah, what could have happened?"

*Kurt—Kurt! I'll kill him myself for this—I will!*

"He's going to die, isn't he?" Meg sobbed, and suddenly Hannah was aware of movement beside her. She opened her eyes and saw Lance's hand rest briefly on Meg's shoulder before pulling away again.

"Not if I can help it," he muttered.

He gave Hannah a curt nod, and she obediently led Meg to the kitchen. She didn't want to watch any more than Meg did, so she took out cold cuts from the fridge and started making sandwiches until she had a whole pile of them on the countertop. Then she stared at all the food and realized that the very thought of eating made her sick.

"What could have happened?" Meg asked again, her voice small and bewildered.

Hannah instantly thought of Kurt's car and Ernie's

body in the trunk. She squeezed her eyes closed and mumbled something under her breath.

"You think it's Kurt, don't you?" Meg persisted. "You don't believe he's hurt anymore, do you? You think he's really out there somewhere, trying to get back at you for breaking up."

"I . . ." Hannah stared at her helplessly. "I think that might be it. Yes." She hesitated, shook her head, sat down slowly in a chair.

"Then where is he?" Meg made a wild gesture toward the back door. "Where could he be hiding all this time? And in all this snow? And how could he do something like that to Bruce?"

Hannah remembered only too well the irrational states of Kurt's anger. She shook her head and stared out the kitchen window.

"I don't know, Meg. I just don't know."

"You think it's Kurt," Meg said again. "And not . . ." Her voice trailed off, and she glanced toward the door to the hall.

"One of the guys?" Hannah finished for her. Again she looked helplessly at her sister, trying to control the quivering in her own voice. "I don't know. I guess . . . one of them could have done it . . . could be pretending to help us . . . getting us to trust him. . . ."

"But which one?" Meg's voice was terrified. "Lance? He's the one who found Bruce—"

"I don't know!"

"But Jonathon's been outside, too! I just can't believe either of them would hurt Bruce! Hannah, I just can't! It's *got* to be Kurt! He *must* be out there somewhere—watching the house—watching *us!* Somehow he knew when I was here alone yesterday—he must have—*Hannah!"*

211

As Meg squealed, Hannah nearly jumped out of her skin. "What is it?"

"The—the chopping sound I dreamed last night—"

Hannah's face went white. She turned quickly to make more sandwiches.

"Maybe it wasn't a dream at all," Meg whimpered. "Maybe someone was chopping—maybe some-one—"

"It *was* a dream," Hannah said fiercely. "You hear me, Meg, it was just a nightmare! You're worn-out and sick and—and"—*Ernie's body in the trunk . . . Ernie stiff and blue and dead*—"with all this happening—" Hannah broke off, fighting for calm. "It was a dream," she said again. "That's all it was."

Tears filmed her eyes, blurring the hazy, white landscape beyond the kitchen window. Her hands trembled, and she felt like she was going to be sick. Quickly she turned and left the room, hurrying away from Meg, away from her own lame excuses, down the hall and out the front door, where she leaned far out over the porch railing and welcomed the shock of wind and snow against her bare, clammy skin.

*A dream . . . a nightmare . . .*

Weakly Hannah lifted her head.

The snowman stood silently on the lawn and gazed back at her.

# 26

"The snow probably saved his life," Lance said matter-of-factly.

He stretched his long legs and leaned back in his chair. He took a sip of the coffee Hannah gave him and glanced anxiously over at Bruce sleeping by the fire.

"If he hadn't been half-buried in it," Lance went on, "he might have bled to death."

"What happened to him?" Hannah asked dully. "I mean, really?"

She and Jonathon and Lance all looked over to where Meg slept on the floor beside Bruce. When Meg had given out a half hour ago, Hannah had covered her with a blanket and left her there.

"Someone gave him a hell of a cut," Lance said. He glanced at Jonathon, then stared down into the steam rising from his cup. "His leg was almost chopped off."

Hannah shuddered. Curled up in a chair, she pulled her knees to her chest and rested her chin on top.

"So," she said quietly, "what do we do about Ernie?"

She and Jonathon had already told Lance about finding the body in the trunk. Now the three of them exchanged silent looks and fixed their eyes on the flickering fire.

"What *can* we do?" Jonathon repeated softly.

"We shouldn't move him," Lance said. "Once the police get here—"

*"If* the police get here," Hannah said glumly.

"If the snow ever stops," Jonathon added, and Lance gave a vacant nod.

"How do you know him?" he asked Hannah.

"He's been our bus driver ever since we moved here," she said sadly. "He always worries about Meg and me being this far outside of town, especially when the weather's bad." She thought a minute, then shook her head. "I don't even know how he died."

"The same way your dog almost died," Jonathon murmured, and she stared at him.

"What? How do you know that?"

"I saw it. When you turned around back there at the car, I . . . saw where he'd been hit."

*Did I turn around? Did Jonathon see into the trunk?* Hannah thought dimly. *Funny . . . I can't even remember.*

"The thing is," Jonathon went on, "when he turns up missing, someone's bound to come looking for him."

In his chair Lance gave a noticeable fidget. He ran one hand back through his hair.

*"If* he told someone he was coming here," Lance said softly. His eyes barely flicked to Hannah. *"Would* he have told anyone he was coming?"

"I don't know," she said truthfully. "I don't think he had a family. I think he lived by himself."

Silence fell heavy around them. Lance stared long and hard into the fire. Hannah could see his hand on the arm of the chair, stroking, stroking in quick, silent gestures.

"Lance?" she asked cautiously.

His eyes remained on the flames. His voice came out in an eerie monotone. "I can't stand that . . . I really can't."

Jonathon looked up in surprise. "Stand what?"

"You know," Lance mumbled. "Defenseless things getting hurt like this. I want to kill the ones who do it."

Hannah felt a chill go through her. She looked at Jonathon, but he only shook his head.

"Kurt's probably miles away by now," he said, not sounding quite convinced. "Just because we found what we found today doesn't mean he's still around."

Lance gave a slow nod. His eyes stayed fixed on the fireplace.

"We don't even know when it happened," Jonathon reminded him.

"Maybe," Lance murmured.

"I just can't believe," Hannah said sadly, "that he'd kill Ernie. No matter how mad he was—"

"Or how drunk?" Jonathon broke in. "Like I said before, suppose Ernie was the one looking in the window at Meg. And suppose Kurt was convinced it was some new boyfriend of yours."

"But he didn't have a ski mask," Hannah insisted again. "Meg said the man at the window had a ski mask."

"He could have lost it. Kurt could have taken it or—"

"Kurt could have been the one with the ski mask," Lance broke in quietly. "Kurt might have been the one looking in."

"But he's probably gone by now," Jonathon repeated, more hopefully this time. "I mean . . . how many ways can you think to terrorize someone?"

"Why did he build the snowman?" Hannah demanded.

Jonathon's eyes darted reluctantly to the closed curtains at the window. Lance kept staring into the fire.

"The snowman," Hannah said again, shifting position on the couch. "It doesn't make sense. Why would he build it out in the yard like that? And nobody heard him? Or saw him?"

"Sick sense of humor," Lance said softly.

"We were all dead tired," Jonathon added. "How could we have heard him?"

*But you weren't dead tired all night,* Hannah thought, and she bit her lip to keep from blurting it out. *Sometime in the night you and Lance both went outside, and I heard you come back in. . . .*

"At least you're thinking about Kurt now and not that escaped killer." Jonathon turned to her with a humorless smile.

Hannah stared at him. Her mind felt numb, her nerves dead. She wanted to show some angry and indignant reaction, but she couldn't summon the strength.

"We're going to need more kerosene," Jonathon pointed out, changing the subject.

Lance nodded. "He's right. I found enough to keep the heaters going so far, but there's not much left."

Hannah's mind groped through a fog. *Was* there any more kerosene? And if so, where would Dad have stored it?

"There must be more in the garage somewhere," she said. "I'll have to go look."

"I'll go with you." Jonathon made a valiant effort to get up, but Lance pushed him back down onto the couch.

"You stay with Meg," Lance said. "You've overdone way too much on that leg already, and you look terrible. I'll go with Hannah."

Hannah looked helplessly from one to the other. She didn't want to be anywhere alone with either of them right now, yet she certainly didn't relish the thought of crossing her own yard all by herself and unprotected. *My own yard . . . my own house . . . and I'm so scared . . .*

For once Jonathon didn't argue, and Hannah squinted through the shadows, trying to see him more clearly. Lance was right—he did look terrible. The dark smudges of pain had deepened below his eyes, giving him a hollow, sunken look. His thin cheeks were the color of paste. Glancing over at Lance, Hannah realized that he was studying Jonathon just as closely.

"Maybe if he could take something," Lance suggested. "It wouldn't hurt him to sleep awhile."

"I don't need anything—" Jonathon began, but Lance broke in more firmly this time.

"Where'd you put those painkillers?"

"In the bathroom," Hannah said. "I'll get them."

"No, that's okay." Jonathon finally managed to heave himself to his feet. "You and Lance go on. I think I can manage a couple pills on my own, thanks very much."

Lance sighed as Jonathon disappeared slowly down the hallway. "I just hope he gets back on the couch before he swallows anything. That way he won't have so far to fall. Come on."

Meg had piled all the coats on a chair in the corner. Hannah dug through and found hers, then paused in the doorway to put on her gloves. She heard Lance pull his jacket from the bottom, then mutter something as Jonathon's coat accidentally slid to the floor.

Lance leaned over and picked it up.

As Hannah turned around, she saw him straighten slowly . . . saw something clutched in his hand. And then, as her eyes focused on his fingers, she saw the hasty movement as he fumbled with Jonathon's pocket.

He tossed Jonathon's coat on the chair.

He'd been quick, but not quick enough.

And as Lance went past her out the door, Hannah looked back at the bulging pocket in Jonathon's coat where Lance had shoved the ski mask back inside.

# 27

*Calm down . . . calm down . . . He said so himself . . . lots of people have ski masks—black ones—Kurt has one, practically everyone at school has one, so what if Jonathon has one, too—*

Hannah argued fiercely with herself as she followed Lance back across the yard. The clouds had opened up again, sending down fresh new flurries, darkening the sky to premature dusk. A violent wind whipped the snow around them, and she put up one arm to shield her face. *Even I have a ski mask. I'm jumping to conclusions. . . . This isn't making any sense—*

She hurried a little, trying to keep up. Lance was getting ahead of her, his long legs slicing a path through the snow, and Hannah stepped where he stepped. As they reached the garage, Lance wrestled the door open and went inside, and Hannah realized they'd forgotten to bring flashlights.

They stood for a minute, eyes trying to adjust to the gloom.

"I can't see a thing," Lance sighed. "Any idea where that kerosene is?"

"Probably somewhere over here. Just give me a second."

Hazy gray light filtered shallowly through the cracks in the walls and beneath the doors. Hannah felt her way along the rear wall and squinted through the shadows. Icy gusts shrieked around the corners of the building, shaking it like a piece of flimsy cardboard.

Something slithered and crashed in the corner beyond the car. Before Hannah could react, Lance was pressed against her, his body wedged between her and the unknown.

She didn't even know she'd been holding her breath till it came out in a long rush.

"What are you doing?" she demanded, shoving him away. "It was just some boxes falling."

For a long moment he said nothing. Then finally his voice spoke through the darkness.

"Where I come from, you listen to every sound. You watch every shadow."

A slow, ragged chill worked through her, though she tried to keep her voice casual. "So where *do* you come from?"

Was that a laugh that sounded so low, so hollow in his throat? Hannah couldn't quite tell, and before she could make up her mind, a heavy thud echoed loudly behind them.

"What was that?" she gasped, but Lance was already working his way past her.

"The door," she heard him mutter. "The wind must have slammed it shut."

Hannah nodded, swallowing hard. She waited while he twisted the knob back and forth and pounded on the wood. When that didn't work, he rattled the knob again, swearing impatiently under his breath.

"Something's jammed it," he said.

"What do you mean?"

"I mean, I can't get it open."

Panic rose into her throat. She tried to choke it back down. "Here—let me try."

Obligingly he stepped aside. Hannah shook the knob for dear life, then used both fists to pound on the door.

"It feels like it's locked!" she said fearfully. "But that's impossible!"

She whirled around to see him staring at her. In the dim light his eyes gleamed with a strange, unsettling calm.

"Well, do something!" she cried.

She backed away from him while he tried the door again. She glanced up at the window on the rear wall, knowing it was too tiny for either of them to squeeze through. Her eyes swept the murky interior of the garage, as though at any second some deranged shadow would separate itself from the others and stalk toward them.

"What about the main one?" Lance asked, motioning to the big door behind the car. But Hannah shook her head.

"It's electric. It won't work."

"Then we'll have to crank it up ourselves."

She nodded and got out of his way. He moved around the car and reached down for the handle at the bottom of the garage door. Giving it a tug, he swore again and glanced back over his shoulder.

"It's no good," he said.

"The snow—it must be the snow." Hannah shifted nervously from one foot to the other. "It's piled up too high outside, isn't it? Against the door?"

"It's not the snow," Lance murmured. He tried again, then stood up slowly to face her. A shadow fell across his face, slicing it jaggedly in half. "The door gives a little, but then it stops. I think something's blocking it from the other side."

"You . . . you mean—"

"Maybe someone wanted us to come out here," Lance said quietly. "Maybe someone didn't want us to come out again."

Hannah's mind reeled. Had it been Jonathon's idea to get kerosene—or Lance's? But Jonathon had offered to come with her—but Lance had tried to get her to stay in the house—or had it been the other way around—

"Kurt," she mumbled. Then louder, "Kurt! It's got to be Kurt doing this—but where the hell *is* he!"

Lance shook his head. Moving back to the smaller door again, he rammed it with his shoulder.

"Help!" Hannah shouted. "Somebody let us out!"

"You might as well save your breath," Lance muttered. "No one can hear you."

He hit the door again, harder. Hannah braced herself for his third try and looked frantically around the garage.

"We'll freeze to death out here! There must be something we can use to get that door open! Come help me look."

Between the dim light and a blindness of growing fear, she couldn't see where anything was—couldn't

222

remember what her father might have handy on the workbench. She started feeling along the counter with her hands, tools clattering onto the floor, her voice irritable as she called back to Lance.

"Did you hear me? Come and help me look for—"

Her words died in her throat. She stopped where she was and stared.

Lance had grown quiet. He was leaning against the door, his face lowered, his palms pressed flat against the wood on either side of his head.

"Lance?" she asked cautiously. "Did you hear me?"

But he didn't seem to have heard anything. He just stood there, not moving, silent as a statue.

"It's not Kurt," he mumbled at last, and this time Hannah reached out for the edge of the worktable and gripped it slowly with cold, cold fingers.

"It's . . . What are you saying?" she murmured.

Ice curdled in her veins. She gripped the table harder and took a deep, shaky breath.

"Lance?" she whispered.

And he was shaking his head now, back and forth against the wall, his long black hair flowing around his shoulders, his voice like deep, smooth velvet.

"No," he whispered, "it never was Kurt. . . ."

Terror filled Hannah's heart. Tears stung her eyes as Lance blurred before her.

"Lance—" she began again, but his head came up, slow and shadowy, and his voice sounded hollow in the darkness of the garage.

"No more lies, Hannah," he said.

"Lance—"

He was coming toward her now . . . step by step . . . and as Hannah backed away from him, she could see the vague movement at his side . . . his hand lifting . . . reaching for her—

She wasn't even aware that she'd picked something up.

Wasn't aware of striking at Lance through the shadows.

She only heard the crack against his skull and saw the crowbar clutched there in her hand, and as she heard him gasp, his body slid sideways down the wall.

*"Help me!"* she screamed.

And she was beating on the door—beating and beating with the crowbar—and as light began to filter in at last, she clawed her way through the splintery opening and tumbled out into the snow.

"Meg—oh, Meg—"

Picking herself up, Hannah raced frantically for the house.

*Did I kill him?—I couldn't have killed him—oh, God, I didn't mean to, but I had to—had to—Jonathon can help—get Meg to safety—all of us away from Lance—*

"Jonathon!" she shouted. *"Meg!"*

She could barely see, the snow was falling so hard. Plowing across the lawn, it seemed to take forever to reach the back porch, and when she finally did, Hannah flung herself against the door, recoiling at once with a look of disbelief.

"Meg!" she screamed. "Jonathon! Unlock the door!"

Again she threw herself against it—again the door held fast.

"Meg! Jonathon! You've got to let me in!"

In desperation Hannah looked down at her empty

hands, realizing she must have dropped the crowbar back at the garage. For a split second she wrestled with the idea of going back for it, then decided not to take the risk. What if she hadn't hit Lance as hard as she thought? There was no telling how long he might be out—even now he might be waking up and coming after her—

*The front door—Jonathon and Meg are probably both in the living room—*

Stumbling down the steps, Hannah made her way along the rear of the house. She'd just reached the back corner when something made her stop, her heart leaping into her throat.

*A movement? Over by the garage?*

She held one hand to her face. She squinted her eyes and wiped flakes from her lashes.

*Someone coming? Or nothing at all?*

Through the steady pouring of snow, it was impossible to tell. . . .

Panic-stricken, Hannah kept on, leaning close to the house, pounding the walls, banging on the downstairs windows. *What's wrong with them—why don't they answer?* She reached the front porch at last and threw herself on the door, shouting hysterically.

*"Meg! Jonathon! Let me in!"*

The door handle wouldn't turn.

"Oh, God, don't you understand? We've got to get out of here!"

Sobbing now, Hannah kicked and beat at the door, her mind on the brink of hysteria. She glanced around wildly for something she could use to break the window, cursing herself for having left the crowbar back at the garage. *A log—that's it—I'll go get a log—*

225

Yet even as she thought it, she knew she couldn't go back—not to the woodpile, not to the other porch—not with Lance back there—

Frantic with terror, she staggered off the porch and out into the yard, screaming Meg's name.

And then she saw the snowman.

It was standing there, watching her.

Staring at her with a sort of smugness on its round, white face . . .

*The shovel!*

Hannah plunged through the snow, stumbling, falling, picking herself up again. And she could see it now—the handle of the shovel—still sticking up ramrod-straight at the snowman's back, the blade thrust down through the base of the snowman's body.

She grabbed the handle and pulled.

For one crazy minute she could almost believe that the snowman was real. That it was pulling back on the shovel, refusing to let go.

Using every ounce of strength, she gave one furious, final tug. The shovel came free so unexpectedly that Hannah toppled off-balance and fell right into the snowman.

To her horror, the whole thing suddenly seemed to explode—snow bursting apart—the head—torso—everything breaking and crumbling around her—

Hannah rolled over, dazed. The shovel lay on top of her, and she was covered with mounds of snow. She sat up carefully, shaking her head, and as her eyes slowly focused on the ground beside her, a scream rose silently into her throat.

There was something inside the snowman.

Something long and bloody and mangled . . . like a twisted entrail hanging from the gash in its stomach

. . . spilling out stiff and frozen across the pure, pure whiteness of the snow . . .

"God . . ." Hannah cried, "oh God . . . *no!*"

For she recognized it now.

She recognized the hideous dead thing staring up at her from the broken shell of the snowman. . . .

It was Kurt.

# 28

Something snapped inside her brain.

Hannah didn't remember getting back to the house —didn't remember breaking the window or climbing inside—didn't remember screaming and screaming until suddenly it occurred to her that her voice was the only sound in the house, and she was standing alone in the living room and her screams were echoing —echoing—but nobody answered—

"Meg!" she cried. "Jonathon!"

Flames hissed and crackled from the hearth. Bruce lay on the floor, not moving.

*My God . . . my God . . . where are they*—

"Meg!" Hannah screamed again. "Jonathon— where *are* you! We've got to get out of here!"

The house yawned around her, still and cold and quiet.

"Somebody . . . somebody please help me," Hannah whispered. She turned to the broken window. Snow billowed into the room, through jagged glass and ripped curtains. *Maybe they've gone to the road— or maybe, somehow, they knew to get away and—*

"Jonathon!" she sobbed. "Meg!"

A gust of wind shook the house. A loose shutter banged. Overhead a floorboard creaked softly.

"Meg?"

Hannah dashed upstairs, going frantically from room to room, finding all of them empty. The house mocked her with its silence, like something in a dream . . . something dead. There was no sign of anyone anywhere. Coming back down, Hannah made a quick search of the first floor and ended up in the kitchen. She unlocked the back door and jerked it open, gazing out through the swirling flakes in the direction of the garage.

Was Lance still out there?

As Hannah strained her eyes, she wondered for the second time if she'd seen a movement in the yard. *Someone creeping toward the house . . . or just a trick of the wind?* How close would he be able to get before she could spot him through all the snow? she wondered.

She slammed the door and snapped the bolt into place. She whirled around and pressed her back against the rough surface of the wood. And then she saw Meg's tissue on the kitchen floor.

Hannah stared.

*That tissue wasn't there when I went to the garage. . . . I don't remember it being there when I left . . . so that means Meg's been in here since then. . . .*

She couldn't move. For endless seconds the kitchen seemed to fade around her . . . to disappear . . . only Meg's crumpled tissue left behind to focus on.

Meg's tissue . . .

And the red drops spattered beside it.

In slow motion Hannah walked forward. Her eyes followed the trail of dark red droplets across the linoleum . . . past the counters . . . to the door of the storeroom. . . .

She could see now, that door wasn't quite closed.

*But why? No one's been in there—the door's never open. . . .*

Her heart leapt into her throat. She choked down her terror and took one more cautious step.

"Meg?" she whispered. "Jonathon?"

She knew they couldn't hear her. She knew the whisper had only been in her head, that her lips were strangely frozen, that her body was like a robot moving mechanically across the floor. . . .

Her eyes fastened on the crack between the wall and the storeroom door. Just a tiny crack. Barely a fraction of an inch. *But nobody ever uses that storeroom. . . .*

"Meg . . . Jonathon . . ."

Slowly Hannah peeled off her gloves. She laid one hand against the door.

The wood was cold and cracked. She recoiled from the touch and clenched her fist. Then . . . carefully . . . she touched the door again.

"Meg?"

Hannah stopped. She held her breath.

There was no sound from the other side of that door, but suddenly she didn't want to go in there— didn't want to push it open—didn't want to know—

didn't *ever* want to know, only she *had* to, she knew she didn't have a choice—

"Oh, Meg," she whimpered, and the door was opening now . . . inch by inch . . . and it was creaking —loud and rusty in the horrible, heavy silence— creaking and creaking, on and on. . . .

She made herself step inside. She made herself step over the threshold, but she kept one hand on the door, kept one hand there so she wouldn't run or fall, to make herself face what she had to face—

Meg was huddled in a corner.

Her hands were tied behind her; a rag was knotted around her mouth. Her hair fell over her forehead, and through the matted strands, her eyes were wide with terror.

There was blood on her face.

As Hannah gasped and started forward, Meg gave a muffled cry. Hannah only caught the quick movement from the corner of her eye as an arm shot out and slammed the door behind her.

Screaming, Hannah whirled around.

He was standing in back of her, pressed against the door. He was wearing a denim jacket, and she could see the ski mask, black as the shadows surrounding him, and one arm down at his side, and his long fingers curled tightly around the handle of the axe.

# 29

"Why are you doing this!" Hannah cried.

Without thinking, she started toward him, but as he stiffened and shifted the axe to his other hand, she froze where she stood. She could hear Meg whimpering from behind the gag, and as Hannah darted a frantic look at her, Meg shook her head hysterically.

"Why?" Hannah asked again. Her own tears were choking her—terror and panic and hopelessness exploding inside. For a split second her mind faded, and she saw her mother's smile, heard her father's laugh for the last time.

"You wanted me to trust you!" she insisted, but she wasn't screaming anymore, she was trying to be calm. With supreme effort she fought to get her voice under control, and then she took a step back.

"It was you all along, wasn't it?" Her voice shook violently, fear giving way to anger now. "Sticking up for Lance—saying how impossible it was for an escaped killer to find us out here—saying Kurt was miles and miles away. When did you kill him? The first night?"

And it was unnerving how he just stood there, not saying anything, not moving, not responding—it was all she could do not to leap on him and start beating him, to shake him and kick him and—

"Answer me! You killed Kurt—and you killed Ernie—and you hid Kurt inside the snowman! And you're the one who hurt Bruce, too! You've been picking us off one by one!" She broke off, her tone icy cold. "I won't let you hurt Meg. Do you hear me?"

She never saw the axe move. One second it rested on the floor at his feet—the next it arced through the air with a deadly hiss and slammed into the floor beside her leg.

Hannah jumped back with a cry.

He picked the axe up again.

He swung it into the air.

"Jonathon!" she yelled. "Jonathon, *stop* it!"

Again the blade sliced down through the floor. He took another step toward Hannah, and the axe glided above his head. Hannah felt the swish of air across her cheek and cried out again as the sleeve of her coat ripped away.

"Stop it, Jonathon! *Stop it!*"

Through a blur of terror she saw him stop—saw him suddenly freeze with the axe poised above his head. She could see the rise and fall of his chest, could hear the raspy sound of his breathing through the black wool.

"Please . . . please, Jonathon . . . I liked you so much. Just stop this."

She backed away from him until she could feel Meg

behind her. She knelt down and gathered Meg into her arms.

"Jonathon," Hannah whispered. "Please."

An eternity passed. Hannah watched as the axe hovered in the air above him. Then finally . . . slowly . . . he lowered it down.

"You don't want to kill anyone else," Hannah said softly. "There's been enough killing. Let us help you. We've been nice to you, haven't we? You've shared our house and our food, we've given you clothes—we've never done anything to try and hurt you—"

He was trembling all over.

She couldn't see his eyes, but she knew he was watching her closely.

"Say something," she begged him. And then her voice rose. "Jonathon, *say* something!"

He shook his head.

"Take the mask off," Hannah urged. "Take it off and let's talk. You should lie down on the couch again, so I can check your leg to make sure you're not bleeding. You might have really hurt yourself. Nobody wants you to hurt yourself."

She was babbling, she knew, but she couldn't help it—*normal, act normal, treat him like everything's okay*—

"I don't want you to bleed again," she rushed on, trying to control the quivering in her voice. "I don't want you hurt. I could fix you something to eat. Look—you're cold and so tired. You need to sleep."

She was moving toward him now . . . slowly . . . slowly . . . her hands held out in front of her.

He stood against the wall and waited. He didn't move, and still he didn't speak.

"Please, Jonathon," Hannah tried again. "You've

been a good friend to me—the best kind of friend I could have. You helped me when I was scared. Please let me help you."

She was standing in front of him now. She reached cautiously for the axe, and to her amazement, he let it slide into her hands. Trying not to shudder, she placed the axe on the floor, and then pushed it carefully with her toe into the corner.

"I'm your friend," she said softly. "Jonathon, do you hear me? I'm really your friend."

She reached up for the ski mask.

He was breathing heavier—harsh guttural sounds deep in his throat.

Hannah gently took hold of the mask. She peeled it over his head.

"Jonathon—" she began, but then suddenly the room was full of screams—Meg's muffled ones and Hannah's own—echoing over and over as the ski mask dropped to the floor at Hannah's feet—

She could see Jonathon's face now.

Only it wasn't Jonathon.

It was a man she'd never seen before.

# 30

For a split second of horror, Hannah gaped at him.

The man had no expression at all.

His eyes were dazed and completely blank.

As he slowly lifted his arm, Hannah spun around and dived for the axe.

A well-aimed kick caught her in the side. As she gasped in pain, she was half-conscious of Meg rolling out of her way, and her own hands scrabbling along the floor for the axe handle. She saw the heavy boots come down, and as they stomped mercilessly, agony burst through her fingers.

*"No!"* Hannah screamed.

Only it was more than fear now—it was hate and utter fury.

Again she threw herself at the axe—felt the wooden handle slide uselessly from her grasp as he jerked it out of reach above her. The air hissed as the blade swept beside her head. Meg gave another muffled shriek. Hannah's arm went up, and something sliced ice-hot through her shoulder.

She lunged at his knees. There was a low growl of surprise as he nearly lost his balance.

He swung again. Hannah held on and pulled with all her strength. She heard his body thud down onto the floor, and she scrambled frantically to find the axe.

Without warning, the room seemed to shatter. Hannah felt the floor shaking beneath her—felt arms grab her and toss her roughly on top of Meg. She tried to push herself up again, but things were spinning, groaning, feet scuffling, things falling and being thrown. Instinctively she tried to shield Meg, and as she did, the axe blade chunked down into the floor, missing them both by a fraction of an inch. Through a haze of terror, Hannah saw it wrench free and lift once more into the air.

A horrible cry pierced the room—reverberating through the walls, down into her very soul. It was the cry of something not human.

And then . . . at last . . .

Silence.

Hannah closed her eyes. She pressed Meg tightly against her, trying to calm her sister's hysterical sobs.

"You okay?" a voice asked above her.

Hannah looked up.

Lance was standing slightly off balance, his arms at his sides. He was covered with blood, and as he fought for breath, he ran one wet hand back through his long, black hair.

Hannah got to her knees, but he put a hand on her shoulder.

"Don't," he said tightly. "You don't want to see."

But Hannah had already spotted the bloody heap in the corner . . . the axe handle rising into the air . . . and she knew she'd seen enough.

# 31

"The last thing I remember," Jonathon said, frowning, "was standing in the kitchen. Then there was this sound behind me—this footstep—and I turned around. And for just a split second, I thought . . ." He dropped his eyes and stared into the fire, but Lance looked back at him, unperturbed.

"You thought it was me," Lance finished.

Jonathon took a long sip of coffee, hands trembling around his cup. His face was gaunt and colorless; all the strength seemed to have gone out of him.

"He had that mask on," Jonathon added softly. His gaze shifted to the towel Lance had wrapped around his leg—a new towel already stained with blood.

*He needs a doctor,* Hannah thought numbly. *He's lost too much blood . . . way too much. . . .*

"He tried to kill Jonathon," Meg whispered.

Three pairs of eyes turned to look at her. Her voice was so small, they had to strain to hear.

"When I first ran into the kitchen, I saw the ski mask, and I started screaming. I thought it was Kurt. Jonathon kept yelling at me to run, and the other guy swung the axe at Jonathon's leg."

Hannah shuddered and put her hands to her ears, but Meg went on.

"He pushed Jonathon down the basement steps. I tried to get the back door open, but the guy shoved me away and locked it."

Tears ran silently down Hannah's face. Her shoulder burned beneath its bandage, and she stared down at the blood on her clothes. She felt strangely detached from the conversation around her, from the other people in the room. *Kurt* . . . She closed her eyes and pulled back into the chair and blocked his face from her mind.

"I guess he didn't plan on any interference at that point," Lance said. "He thought Hannah and I were locked in the garage. He thought Jonathon was taken care of." He paused, then glanced over at Meg. "He thought Meg was his next victim."

With an effort Hannah roused and shook her head. "But I still don't understand. Why—"

"His name is Martin Jessup," Lance said flatly. "He killed his whole family in this house twenty years ago."

Jonathon looked incredulous. "How do you know that?"

"I work at Fairway Institution. I've heard him relive that murder over and over. For him, time's never passed since that night. He's like a machine that's been programmed to kill. I always knew he'd go back home if he ever got the chance."

The other three regarded Lance in stunned silence.

"You . . . *knew?*" Jonathon burst out. "You knew it was him all the time?"

Lance kept his eyes on the flames. For a long time he said nothing.

"I *had* been camping when I heard the news report," he said at last. "Some guy ran me off the road, and my car got stuck." He barely glanced at Hannah. "It was Kurt. He offered me a ride. He was so drunk, I wouldn't have gone, but I needed to get to a phone . . . to call in and tell the hospital I was in the area. Then the wreck happened. And when I woke up, I didn't know where I was."

He closed his eyes . . . paused . . . opened them again.

"I didn't realize this was the house. Not till Hannah told you about its history."

Silence stretched out. Meg stirred and touched Lance gently on the shoulder.

"Why'd you stay?" she whispered.

Lance slowly shook his head. "I couldn't leave you two alone. I didn't know what was going to happen—where Jessup really was, or if they'd managed to catch him. And then Kurt came into the picture . . . threatening Hannah. . . ."

He trailed off. Hannah wrapped her arms around her chest, hugging herself tightly, choking back her pain.

"Kurt must have come that night, then," Jonathon murmured, and Lance gave a nod.

"Left the stuff in the station wagon. But what happened after that, we'll never know for sure."

He leaned over and picked up the poker. He stabbed listlessly at the fire.

"My guess is, Kurt got killed that night. Maybe

Jessup hid him—I don't know. The woodpile? The doghouse? But things kept interfering with Jessup's plan. . . ."

"Bruce," Jonathon said softly. "The bus driver."

"It's the fear he likes," Lance mumbled. "Always the fear. He didn't kill them all at once, that night twenty years ago. He dragged it out. He made sure they all knew what was happening to them."

Hannah turned her face in to the cushions. Her heart felt cold and dead inside her.

"Jessup didn't hide in just one place here either, did he?" Jonathon threw Lance a meaningful look. "The garage? The woods? Even the doghouse again—"

"The storeroom," Lance muttered, and Meg gasped in alarm.

"He was *here?* In the *house?*"

Hannah heard her through a deep fog. *Footsteps in the house . . . missing food . . . Meg's bear . . . shadows in the hallway . . . My God, he was here all the time. . . .*

"The noises we heard," Jonathon spoke up again. "It was him, wasn't it? Playing with us. We'd go out to look, but we never found anything." At Lance's nod, he went on. "We were afraid to leave you two alone in the house. So I'd keep watch by the porch, while Lance went out to investigate. I thought it was Kurt."

"I didn't want to panic anyone." Lance sounded almost defensive. "Especially with Hannah so upset about the escaped killer."

Voices grew still once more. Flames crackled up the chimney, and logs sputtered quietly to ash. Hannah gazed at the window where Lance had nailed boards over the broken glass. Someone had drawn the curtains closed again. She could see their faint rustling as wind crept through the cracks.

"So . . . what do we do now?" Meg's voice trembled.

"I guess we wait," Jonathon murmured. "Wait for help to come."

Hannah sank lower into her chair. Outside the wind howled mournfully, and night fell, deep and black.

"It's snowing harder," Meg said.

Vacantly Hannah wondered what morning would bring. Kurt would never see it. Neither would Ernie . . . or Martin Jessup lying out there in the garage . . .

She saw Jonathon get up from the couch. He crossed the room and eased down beside her on the arm of her chair. Meg buried her face in her hands. Lance gazed hard into the fire.

Beside the hearth, Bruce stirred and lifted his head, whining softly.

The flames roared up as a cold draft swept the room.

"What's that?" Meg whispered, and Hannah felt Jonathon tense—saw Meg's huge eyes—watched Lance hesitate, then slip noiselessly into the hall.

And "It's all right," Jonathon kept saying, "it's all right—" over and over, trying to calm her, even as Lance motioned for quiet and turned slowly, slowly to face them. . . .

"Listen," he mumbled. "Someone's at the door."

# About the Author

Richie Tankersley Cusick loves to read and write scary books. Richie enjoys writing when it is rainy and gloomy outside, and likes to have a spooky soundtrack playing in the background. She writes at a desk that originally belonged to a funeral director in the 1800s and that she believes is haunted. Halloween is one of her favorite holidays. She and her husband decorate the entire house, which includes having a body laid out in state in the parlor, life-size models of Franken-stein's monster, the figure of Death to keep watch, and a scary costume for Hannah, their dog. A neighbor recently told them that a previous owner of the house was feared by all of the neighborhood kids and no one would go to the house on Halloween.

Richie is the author of *Vampire, Fatal Secrets, The Locker, The Mall, Silent Stalker, Help Wanted, The Drifter, Someone at the Door,* and the novelization of *Buffy, the Vampire Slayer,* in addition to several adult novels for Pocket Books. She and her husband, Rick, live outside Kansas City, where she is currently at work on her next novel.